**'Believe me, the last thing I want—or need—is a man in my life,' Bethany said firmly.**

Well, that was certainly clear enough. Michael knew he should have left it there, but something impelled him to observe, 'That's a bit definite, isn't it?'

'I can be definite, Michael. I've got my children, my work, and a new home. I can change a plug, mend a fuse, put up bookshelves—'

'Men have other uses apart from DIY, Bethany.'

D1079964

**Maggie Kingsley** lives with her family in a remote cottage in the north of Scotland, surrounded by sheep and deer. She is from a family with a strong medical tradition, and has enjoyed a varied career, including lecturing and working for a major charity, but writing has always been her first love. When not writing, she combines working for an employment agency with her other interest, interior design.

**Recent titles by the same author:**

FOR JODIE'S SAKE

# JUST
# GOOD FRIENDS

BY
MAGGIE KINGSLEY

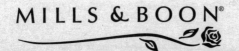

MILLS & BOON®

*All the characters in this book have no existence outside the imagination of the author, and have no relation whatsoever to anyone bearing the same name or names. They are not even distantly inspired by any individual known or unknown to the author, and all the incidents are pure invention.*

*MILLS & BOON and MILLS & BOON with the Rose Device are registered trademarks of the publisher.*

*First published in Great Britain 2000
Harlequin Mills & Boon Limited,
Eton House, 18-24 Paradise Road, Richmond, Surrey TW9 1SR*

© Maggie Kingsley 2000

ISBN 0 263 82282 6

*Set in Times Roman 10½ on 11¼ pt.
03-0101-51449*

*Printed and bound in Spain
by Litografía Rosés, S.A., Barcelona*

# CHAPTER ONE

'MICHAEL—Michael, hold up there a minute. I need to talk to you!'

Michael Harcus turned with a frown, then his lips twitched as he saw his sister Connie driving into the Harbour Medical Centre car park.

'You could have saved yourself a trip, Connie,' he declared after she'd fought her way out of her ancient Land Rover, despite the best efforts of her boisterous cocker spaniel to prevent her. 'Simon's already told me about your barbecue tomorrow night, and I've got plans for this weekend.'

'Sailing alone in that silly boat of yours?' His sister thrust a hand through her blonde curls, making them even more dishevelled than they already were, and shook her head. 'Come to my barbecue. You'll enjoy it more.'

'Frankly, I think I'd prefer to have my toenails pulled out one by one,' he said dryly. 'Look, Connie, why don't you just give it up?'

'Give what up?' she asked, her large blue eyes wide and innocent.

'Your matchmaking.'

'I'm not—'

'Connie, there isn't a single unattached woman on Orkney you haven't invited to dinner or to a barbecue on my behalf, and the only thing you've done is increase my waistline.'

'Rubbish,' she retorted, her eyes skimming over her brother's muscular six-foot-two-inch frame. 'And, anyway, Bethany Seton's not single, she's divorced.'

His eyebrows snapped down. 'Bethany Seton?'

Damn. She'd never intended telling him she'd invited
Bethany to the barbecue but it was too late now. 'You've
heard of her?' she asked, deliberately casual.

Oh, Michael had heard of her all right. In fact, just lately
it seemed as though everyone he met was talking about the
herbalist who'd moved into Sorrel Cottage two months ago.
And he could just imagine what she looked like. All flowing hair, home-made skirts and open-toed sandals. Very
New Age. Very alternative medicine.

'Connie, if you think for one minute that I'd have anything in common with a dispenser of quack potions and
even more dubious massage treatments, you need your head
examined,' he said tightly.

For a second his sister gazed uncertainly at him, then
cleared her throat. 'Michael, I know you still feel very
badly about Amy Wylie—'

'*Badly!*' he exclaimed, only to bite his lip when he saw
his sister's expression. 'Connie, she'd be alive today if that
charlatan she went to on the mainland hadn't talked her
into trying his useless potions.'

'You don't know that for sure—'

'Connie, I've been a GP for ten years and if there's one
thing I *do* know it's that two children wouldn't have been
left motherless if Amy had let me treat her cancer, instead
of choosing to go to a quack herbalist.'

'Bethany isn't a quack.'

'No?' His eyebrows rose cynically.

'No,' she retorted. 'She's got certificates and everything,
and I think you'd like her if you met her.'

'And if you believe that then you've been out in the sun
too long.'

'That's what Simon said,' she admitted. 'Only a lot more
colourfully.'

Michael grinned. His sister's husband would. In fact,
Simon Robson had turned out to be the perfect medical
partner—calm, dependable, with a good sense of humour—

nd any qualms Michael might have felt about going into
partnership with a man who was also his brother-in-law had
disappeared within days of them working together.

'Then I suggest you listen to your husband in future,' he
declared, 'and accept I'm perfectly happy as I am.'

'Rattling around in that big empty house of yours, sailing
alone every weekend you can? Michael, I have never in-
terfered in your private life...' she ignored his hoot of de-
rision '...but you're not getting any younger—'

'Thanks a lot.'

'And if you're not careful you're going to turn into a
crusty, crotchety old bachelor. You're thirty-six years old,
and it's been two years since you dated anyone—'

'Not that you're counting.'

*'Michael!'*

'OK, OK!' He laughed as his sister glared at him. 'But,
Connie, the day I need you to choose a girlfriend for me
is the day I sign myself into a nursing home.'

He was right, of course, his sister thought impotently. In
fact, with his thick, golden brown hair, deeply cleft chin
and impossibly broad shoulders, he could have taken his
pick, and yet since Sarah Taunton had left Orkney two
years ago he'd dated no one.

'Michael, about Sarah...'

'I thought we were talking about Bethany Seton and your
barbecue?'

Connie only just stopped herself from stamping her foot
as she gazed up into her brother's suddenly shuttered face.
It was always the same. Every time she tried to get him to
talk about Sarah, she got the same blank wall of silence.

And it didn't make any sense. From the little she'd seen
of the two of them together she'd never have said Sarah
had been the great love of his life, but when Sarah had left
her PR job at the Flotta Oil Terminal and gone back down
south Michael had changed.

Slowly, almost imperceptibly, he'd ceased to date,

ceased even to attend any social functions, until the man who'd once had the reputation for discarding his girlfriend with as little thought as he'd discarded his expensive suit had become known as the man who never went anywhere.

'Michael—'

'Who else is coming to this barbecue of yours apart from your New Age traveller?'

'What's the point in telling you if you're not going to be there?' she exclaimed tartly. 'And I don't care what you say. I *like* Bethany. She has two of the cutest children you've ever seen—Katie, who's six, and Alistair, who's ten—'

'Oh, Connie...'

She held up her hand quickly, seeing the concern in his face, and smiled a little crookedly. 'It doesn't upset me any more—truly it doesn't. I can see women with children—'

'Connie, let me send you for more tests.'

'Michael, I've seen more specialists than I care to remember and they've all said the same thing. I've got unexplained infertility and at thirty-two the chances of me conceiving are minuscule.'

'Connie—'

'Which is why I think it's about time you got round to carrying on the family name.'

He burst out laughing. 'No way, Connie, not ever. Confirmed bachelor, that's me.'

'You're certainly a confirmed something!' she flared.

He grinned. 'But you still love me.'

His sister stared at him silently for a moment, then sighed. 'I do, which is why I want you to be happy with someone, like Simon and me.'

His lips quirked. 'OK, Connie, it's a deal. When I find someone like Simon, I promise I'll marry him.'

She opened her mouth then closed it again, and this time she did stamp her foot. 'Oh, you...you're impossible!'

'Connie—'

She whirled on her heel and got back into her car. 'I have to go. You may not be coming to my barbecue tomorrow night but if I don't get into town soon the only thing my guests will be eating is sausages.'

'Connie, wait—'

But she didn't wait. She drove out of the car park without a backward glance, and Michael's smile faded as he watched her.

His sister meant well, he knew she did, but...

Once, a long time ago now, he'd pictured himself with a wife and family. Once he'd been so deeply in love he'd have thought the world well lost so long as Lorraine had been safe. Lorraine, who had made him blissfully happy when he'd been doing his pre-registration year at the Aberdeen Infirmary until he'd come home one night to find her gone.

She'd left a note, of course, he remembered, his mouth twisting into a bitter parody of a smile as he got into his car. A note that had told him she'd been fed up with him falling into bed exhausted every night. Fed up with him constantly studying, fed up with never having any money, fed up with him.

And it had been then that he'd started flitting from girl-friend to girlfriend, backing off as soon as any of the girls had become too intense, until Sarah had confronted him with some unpalatable home truths.

'I don't know who the girl was who made you so afraid of commitment, Michael, and I don't care,' she'd said as she'd packed her bags. 'All I do know is that I'm walking out on you before I do something really stupid, like falling in love with you—and that's the last thing you want, isn't it? You want the chase, the conquest, but not the involvement. I'd pity you if I thought you could be hurt but you don't have a heart any more.

'Oh, you have an organ that pumps blood through your body, but a heart that cares, a heart that would give itself to someone else—for someone else? No, I don't think you've had that for a very long time.'

He'd been furious, livid, he remembered as he drove into Albert Street, but the more he'd thought about what Sarah had said, the more he'd realised she'd been right. It had been then he'd vowed there would be no more dates, no more casual relationships, and if that meant he was destined to turn into a crotchety old bachelor, so be it. At least no more women like Sarah would be badly hurt when their relationship ended.

'Dr Harcus—Dr Harcus!'

George Abbot was waving to him from among the shoppers thronging Albert Street, and Michael brought his car to a halt. The retired fisherman had suffered from chronic pain in his knees for the last five years and neither the painkillers nor the anti-inflammatory drugs Michael had prescribed for his arthritis had helped. Giving him steroids had been very much a last-ditch hope but, judging from the beaming smile on the fisherman's face as he walked towards him, it seemed as though they were working.

'You're looking well, George,' Michael observed, rolling down his window. 'The steroids suiting you, are they?'

'Haven't been taking them, Doctor. Leastwise I did, then I stopped.'

'George, I said it was vital to take the whole course—'

'Aye, I know, but the wee lassie prescribed something else.'

Michael's eyebrows rose in confusion. 'The wee lassie?'

'Mrs Seton—the herbalist out at Evie. She didn't do nothing radical, Doctor,' George continued, as an odd expression appeared in Michael Harcus's eyes, an expression hard to interpret but distinctly disquieting. 'Well, perhaps the cabbage leaves are a bit odd—'

'The cabbage leaves?'

'I have to iron them first, then put them on my knees while they're still hot. Aye, I thought it sounded queer, too.' George nodded as Michael's lip curled. 'But it really does help, and the herbs she's given me have done wonders.'

'Have they?' Michael's smile was tight.

'I don't want you to think I'm not grateful for all the treatment you've given me, Doctor,' George continued, his weather-beaten face creased with anxiety, 'but your pills—they never seemed to do no good. Whereas Mrs Seton... Well, I've not been able to walk as far as Albert Street in years.'

Michael all but ground his teeth as he rolled up the window. Bethany Seton doing the odd bit of massage on one of his patients was one thing. If people had money to waste, and were gullible enough to believe she was helping them, so be it, but if she was countermanding his treatments, prescribing her own quack remedies...

It was high time he paid Bethany Seton a visit, he decided. Connie would have said it was the neighbourly, friendly thing to do. Blow the friendly, neighbourly bit, he thought grimly. What Bethany Seton needed right now was to be taken down a peg or two, and he was just in the mood to do it.

'Oh, hellfire, blast and damnation!' Bethany Seton exclaimed as a rush of dirty water poured out from under her kitchen sink onto the floor.

'Mummy! You just said some very naughty words!'

Mummy would like to have said a good deal lot more, Bethany thought ruefully as she sat back on her heels and surveyed the mess. Mummy would like to personally throttle the idiot who'd written the *DIY Guide to Every Household Task*, which had made unblocking a sink sound like child's play. Now not only did she have a blocked sink, she had a flooded floor as well.

'Alistair, could you phone the plumber for me?' she said wearily. 'His number's on my desk—'

'I want to phone,' Katie protested as her brother turned to go. 'I was the one helping with the sink so I should be the one who phones.'

'You're too little to do it,' Alistair declared with all the lofty superiority of his ten years. 'You'd only get it wrong.'

'Would not!'

'Would, too!'

'Mummy, tell him I wouldn't get it wrong, tell him—'

'Katie, would you just let Alistair phone Mr Duncan before the whole house is flooded?'

Her daughter's small chin wobbled for a second, then she flew out of the kitchen on a sob, and as Alistair followed her, his face a silent mask of reproof, Bethany swore again under her breath.

She hadn't meant to be so sharp but...

More expense. Just when she'd thought she might actually be starting to get on top of things, she was going to have more expense. Plumbers didn't come cheap. Twenty pounds an hour was about average, and that was only for their time.

Tears burned at her throat and she gulped them down quickly. Feeling sorry for herself wasn't going to solve anything. Feeling sorry for herself wasn't going to get her anywhere.

'Mummy—Mr Duncan's here!' Katie shrieked at the top of her lungs from her bedroom.

Good grief, that was quick. Either the plumber had been working in the neighbourhood or the man had wings.

'And he hasn't come in a van,' Katie continued, awe and admiration plain in her voice. 'He's come in a huge big car!'

Not wings but a huge big car. Oh, great. Make his time £25 an hour minimum, Bethany sighed, abandoning her mop and bucket.

Maybe he might allow her to pay his bill in instalments? Better yet, perhaps she could offer him a course of free massages in lieu of payment? On second thoughts, no. Men tended to get that look in their eye when you mentioned massage. That look that suggested seedy hotel rooms, whips and girls dressed as nannies.

She sighed again and went slowly over to the window, only to blink as Robert Duncan got out of his car. Connie had said he was the best plumber on the island but what she'd neglected to mention had been that he was also tall, muscular and quite impossibly good-looking.

No wonder he could afford to drive a gleaming red Mercedes, Bethany thought waspishly as her gaze took in his deeply cleft chin and golden brown hair. His male clients were probably too intimidated by his height to query his bills, while his female clients were probably too busy drooling over him to even think about it.

Well, as a thirty-three-year-old divorcee living on a shoe-string, she wasn't going to be influenced by a handsome face, she decided as she went out of the kitchen and down the hall to greet him. When Robert Duncan's bill arrived it would be examined with a fine-toothed comb.

Michael shook his head as he gazed at Sorrel Cottage. It had been weeks since he'd been over to this part of Orkney and the cottage had looked pretty dilapidated then. It didn't look a whole lot better now.

The garden was a wilderness, the house had an unloved, uncared-for appearance, and the only real sign of life was the incongruous appearance of a pink and white tricycle abandoned on the weed-strewn gravel path. That, and the fact that the front door was open.

For a second he hesitated. There was a doorbell, which looked so rusty he doubted if it would work, and a knocker he strongly suspected would come off in his hand if he tried to lift it. Well, the door was open, he reminded himself as he stepped into the hall and came to a very fast halt as a large, hairy dog of indeterminate breed came careering towards him, barking at the top of its lungs.

'It's all right—he won't harm you!' a feminine voice called as Michael involuntarily took a step back. 'Friend, Tiny—*friend*!'

Tiny was neither small nor did he look as though he would understand the concept of friendship, and Michael braced himself for the onslaught, but to his amazement the dog slewed to a halt and immediately sat down.

'He's really a big softy at heart,' the feminine voice continued. 'All noise and bluster, but there's not an ounce of badness in him.'

As if to confirm the observation Tiny began wagging his tail, but his friendly overture was wasted. Michael's gaze was fixed on the woman walking towards him, the woman dressed in a paint-spattered boiler suit and equally paint-daubed wellingtons.

The only thing he'd been right about had been her hair, he realised. It was long, and thick, and auburn, and, though not flowing about her shoulders, as he'd predicted, but gathered up into a French pleat, it was quite clearly winning the battle against the combs which held it.

That much he saw and registered but what he hadn't expected—could never have anticipated—was the lurch his heart suddenly gave as he stared down into a pair of the largest grey eyes he'd ever seen.

If he'd been a fanciful man he would have said fate had just tapped him on the shoulder. If he'd been a romantic he would have called it destiny. But he was neither of these things and as the smile on Bethany Seton's face faded, to be replaced by a look of uncertainty, he pulled himself together quickly.

'Mrs Seton?' he hazarded, hoping he might be wrong.

'That's me,' she replied, her smile returning. 'Thank you so much for coming so quickly.'

'So quickly?' He frowned. 'Mrs Seton—'

'It's through here,' she continued, leading the way past a collection of wellingtons, tennis rackets and abandoned toys. 'I'm hoping I've simply got an air-lock, but—'

'Mrs Seton…' He paused and glanced down, feeling the squelch of water beneath his feet. 'Your floor's flooded.'

'I tried to unblock it myself. It looked so easy in the book, but…' She shrugged. 'As you can see, it wasn't.'

'I've always found it better to leave jobs like that to the expert,' he observed. 'It can end up costing you twice as much otherwise.'

Oh, Lord, that sounded ominous, but the sink had to be fixed—and quickly. Perhaps she could ask Mardi to take a cut in her hours? No, she couldn't do that. Employing a receptionist might seem like an extravagance but without one she'd always be breaking off in the middle of consultations to answer the phone. She'd just have to economise somewhere else. On something.

'Can you start right away?' she asked. 'I'm expecting a patient in an hour, you see, and—'

'Start?' he repeated, his frown returning.

'With unblocking the sink.'

'The sink?'

Ye gods, the man might be handsome enough to give a weaker woman sleepless nights but he was also as thick as two short planks.

'It's the reason I called you out, Mr Duncan,' she said carefully. 'The floor's just an added extra.'

The penny dropped. 'Mrs Seton, I'm Michael Harcus. Dr Michael Harcus from the Harbour Medical Centre in Kirkwall?' he added helpfully when it was her turn to gaze at him in confusion.

'Then this is a *social* call,' she exclaimed with a deep throaty chuckle that seemed to curl down deep inside him. 'Oh, I'm so sorry. Please, sit down— On second thoughts, no, at least not in here. Come through to the sitting room—'

'Mrs Seton—'

'Would you like some coffee—tea?'

'Mrs Seton—'

'I'm babbling, aren't I—not letting you get a word in edgewise?' She laughed again. 'I'm sorry—what did you want to say?'

She was smiling up at him, her large grey eyes warm, expectant, and as an answering smile was irresistibly drawn from him the thought of launching into the diatribe he'd been rehearsing all the way over in the car no longer appealed.

She looked so much more vulnerable than he'd expected for a start. She might be the mother of two, and more gently rounded than fashionably slender, but there was an air of fragility about her he found oddly touching. Perhaps it was her lack of height—five feet three inches tops, he guessed. Perhaps it was the dark shadows under her amazing eyes and those other deeper shadows that lurked inside them, which spoke of unhappiness and heartache.

And she's also the woman who told George Abbot to stop taking his steroids. The reminder hit him like a bolt from the blue and his smile vanished.

'I wouldn't exactly describe my visit as a social call, Mrs Seton,' he said, his mouth compressed. 'More an opportunity to give you a friendly word of warning. Stop poaching my patients.'

'Stop poaching…?' Bewilderment was plain on her face. 'What patient? Who are you talking about?'

'George Abbot—retired fisherman—arthritis in his knees? You told him to stop taking the steroids I prescribed.'

'I would never tell a patient—'

'You spun him some mumbo-jumbo rubbish about the healing power of cabbage leaves—'

'Now, just hold on there a minute,' she interrupted, two bright spots of colour suddenly staining her too-pale cheeks. 'Number one, I would never advise a patient to stop taking medication prescribed by their doctor—*ever*! And number two, herbalism is not mumbo-jumbo. People have been using herbs to treat their illnesses for thousands of years—'

'And killing themselves off in the process. Rosemary can cause miscarriages in pregnant women, fennel can bring on epileptic fits in the susceptible—'

'And orthodox medicine has given us Thalidomide children, Valium addicts and foetal anticonvulsant syndrome in children born to epileptic mothers who were given carbamazepine to control their epilepsy. I suggest that before you start attacking my profession, Dr Harcus, you remember that your own branch of medicine has had its fair share of disasters!'

She was right—he knew she was—and that knowledge only made him angrier. OK, she might have the sort of eyes a man could feel he'd never tire of gazing into, and lips that were full and soft and moist-looking, but, damn it, when you came right down to it she was nothing more than a quack. And a potentially dangerous one at that.

'Mrs Seton, I did not come here to…to bandy words with you about my profession,' he exclaimed tightly, vainly attempting to sidestep Tiny who seemed to have developed an inordinate interest in the contents of his jacket pockets.

'No, you came here—walked in uninvited, I might add—to accuse me of stealing your patients,' she flared. 'I do not drag people off the street into my home, Dr Harcus. They come to see me of their own free will, and I refuse to send them away simply because you're too narrow-minded and prejudiced to accept that I might actually be able to help them!'

'Oh, and I'm sure you can always help them,' he said, his voice dripping with sarcasm. 'Especially when it's in your own best interests financially to do so.'

Her grey eyes flashed fierily, but when she spoke it was with icy calm. 'Believe it or not—and I'm sure you won't—I happen to think there are more important things in life than a vast bank account. If I can't help someone, if I discover there's something wrong with them—something that worries me—I always tell them to see their own doctor.'

His eyebrows rose. 'And how—exactly—would you know if there was something wrong with them, Mrs Seton? Do you use tarot cards in your diagnosis, or perhaps you prefer to consult a crystal ball?'

She clenched her hands together tightly, knowing it was only her innate good manners and his sheer height which were stopping her from slapping the arrogant sneer off his handsome face.

'I'm a fully qualified herbalist and aromatherapist, Dr Harcus, with a B.Sc. honours degree in herbal medicine from Middlesex University. Yes, I thought that might surprise you…' She nodded as his jaw dropped. 'And all I can say is your assumption that I'm a quack and a charlatan says a helluva lot more about you than it does about me!'

'Mrs Seton—'

'I'd be obliged if you'd close the door on your way out. Leaving it open seems to be attracting all sorts of undesirable visitors.'

He opened his mouth, closed it again and strode, whitelipped, to the kitchen door.

'Thought of something else you'd like to accuse me of, have you?' she said tartly, as he suddenly halted and delved first into one pocket of his jacket, then the other. 'I mean, why stop at accusing me of poaching your patients, why not—?'

'My mobile phone—it's gone.'

'Are you implying I *stole* it?' she asked in disbelief.

'Not you—your dog. He was sniffing about my pockets—'

'Dr Harcus, my dog is not a thief. My dog would never—'

'I saw him taking it out into the garden, Mummy. I think he was going to bury it.'

The communicator of this information was a small, slender girl with large grey eyes and auburn hair. Katie Seton, Michael decided. With that hair and those eyes she couldn't be anybody else.

'I...I'm sure he can't have taken it very far,' Bethany said quickly as Michael threw her a look which spoke volumes. 'I'll get it back for you—I promise I will.'

Well, this was just wonderful, terrific, Michael thought, fuming inwardly as she disappeared before he could stop her. He'd planned to be out on his boat by seven, and now he was going to be stuck here for God knew how long while Bethany Seton chased her dog around the garden.

'You don't look very much like a plumber to me.'

He turned to see that Katie Seton had been joined by a blond-haired boy of about ten—a blond-haired boy whose large grey eyes were fixed on him with deep suspicion.

'That's probably because I'm not a plumber,' Michael replied, dredging up a smile. After all, it wasn't these poor kids' fault that their mother was an idiot. 'I'm Dr Harcus, and you, I think, must be Alistair.'

'How did you know his name?' the little girl asked in amazement.

'Because I was told that the prettiest girl in Evie was called Katie and the smartest boy there was called Alistair.'

Katie giggled, but her brother, Michael noticed, merely intensified his scrutiny.

'I'm six,' Katie volunteered, coming forward a step. 'How old are you?'

'Mum says it's rude to ask people personal questions.' Her brother scowled.

'Asking somebody how old they are isn't rude,' Katie protested. 'People are always asking me how old I am.'

Michael hid a smile. 'I'm thirty-six.'

'That's old,' she declared after some consideration.

'That's older than Mummy. That's older than Mrs Weston who sells us goat's milk. That's even older than—'

'Where do you go to school?' Michael interrupted, deciding he felt quite geriatric enough already.

'Evie Primary School, but we're on holiday now. Where do your children go to school?'

'I don't have any children.'

A frown appeared on Katie's small face. 'Don't you like children?'

'Of course I like children,' Michael replied, and he did— at least in the abstract. He didn't like the ones who raced about the surgery while their mothers attempted to explain that the little darlings were actually quite ill despite all the evidence to the contrary. And he certainly didn't like the ones who let out sudden shrieks in the supermarket just as he reached for a bottle of his favourite wine, but in general he was pretty convinced that he liked children. 'Yes, I like children,' he repeated. 'I just don't happen to have any.'

'Why not?'

'Because...because...' Michael tugged at his shirt collar which suddenly felt too tight. There was something oddly nerve-racking about a child's critical stare, and when two children were doing it... 'Look, why don't we go and see if your mum has found my mobile phone yet?'

He'd got as far as the hall when Bethany Seton appeared, looking decidedly red-cheeked and dishevelled.

'I've got your phone but I'm afraid it seems to be a little damaged.' God, that had to be the biggest understatement of the year, she thought ruefully as she held out the mangled remains to him. 'I will, of course, reimburse you for the cost of a new one.'

'I should hope so,' he replied acidly, 'and as quickly as possible, if you please.'

'Naturally,' she declared, her tone every bit as haughty as his, though quite where she was going to find the money to replace his phone she couldn't imagine. 'Now, if you could see yourself out…?'

Oh, he could see himself out, he decided as he strode furiously down the hall. In fact, if he never saw Bethany Seton and her damn dog again it would be too soon, but as he slammed the front door shut behind him he heard an ominous clatter. The rusty doorknocker had fallen off and was lying at his feet.

For a second he stared down at it. Nobody would ever know it was his fault. If he kicked it into the scrub that masqueraded as a front garden he very much doubted if anyone would even miss it, and yet…

With a muttered oath he gritted his teeth and banged on the door with his fist.

It opened in seconds and Bethany Seton gazed up at him coolly. 'Did you forget something? A dry-cleaning bill for dog hairs on your jacket? A cobbler's bill for water damage to your shoes?'

'I believe this is yours,' he said, holding out the doorknocker to her before producing a twenty-pound note from his pocket. 'Buy another with my compliments.'

She looked down at the money in his hand, then up at him, her face expressionless. 'That was an antique doorknocker, Dr Harcus.'

In a pig's ear it was an antique. He knew it, and he was damn sure she knew it, too, and a tide of livid colour swept across his cheeks.

How had this visit gone so badly wrong? He'd driven out here with a perfectly legitimate complaint, and by now most women in Bethany Seton's position would have been reduced to a gibbering mass of apologies. Yet he was the one who felt like a fool and, worst of all, he strongly suspected he looked it.

'Perhaps we should call our debts quits, Mrs Seton,' he said tightly. 'One state-of-the-art mobile phone for one…one antique doorknocker.'

She actually had the gall to appear to have to consider his suggestion before agreeing to it, but what made him angry—far angrier than he'd ever been in his life—was that as he drove away he could hear the all-too-clear sound of her laughter following him.

# CHAPTER TWO

'Oh, I wish I'd been here, Bethany, I really do!' Connie exclaimed, wiping the tears of laughter from her eyes. 'Just to see Michael's face when you told him your doorknocker was an antique!'

Bethany laughed, too, but her laughter held more than a trace of uncertainty. 'Connie...your brother...is he likely to bear a grudge?'

'I think he's probably sticking pins into a wax effigy of you even as we speak!'

'Connie—'

'He deserved it, Bethany. Waltzing into your home un-invited, trying to intimidate you. It's high time Michael was taken down a peg or two, and I'm only sorry I wasn't here to see it.' She got to her feet. 'And now I really must go. I've a million things to do before my barbecue tonight. You are still coming, aren't you?'

'Wouldn't miss it,' Bethany replied brightly, but she couldn't prevent a small sigh from springing to her lips as she waved Connie goodbye then went along to the small office she'd created out of one of the downstairs bedrooms.

It was all very well for Connie to say her brother needed taking down a peg or two—and Bethany couldn't deny she'd relished every minute of it—but the more she thought about what she'd done, the more she realised she'd probably made the biggest professional mistake of her life.

The herbalist she'd worked for in Winchester had always been on excellent terms with the local doctors. In fact, they'd routinely referred patients to him for conditions that conventional medicine could do little to ease, but the chances of Michael Harcus doing that for her now were nil.

And if he took it into his head to actively dissuade his patients from consulting her…

'You look as though you've just lost a pound and found a penny,' her receptionist declared, smiling up at her from behind her desk.

'Something like that,' Bethany replied ruefully. 'I'm just wondering how much Mr Duncan is going to charge me for unblocking my sink.'

'You should have asked Dr Harcus to take a look at it for you when he was here,' Mardi observed. 'I understand he's very good with his hands.'

And probably downright incredible with the rest of his anatomy, Bethany thought, suddenly finding herself remembering how broad his shoulders had been, and as for his muscular thighs…

'Isn't Michael just too good-looking for words?' Mardi continued dreamily, as though she'd read Bethany's mind. 'Those deep brown eyes of his, that cute cleft chin—'

'I thought you were supposed to be marrying Eric Foubister in October?' Bethany said.

'I am, but just because I've made my selection from the candy store it doesn't mean I can't admire the rest of the goods,' Mardi protested, then her plump face lit up. 'You know, Michael would be just perfect for you. No, listen,' she continued as Bethany let out a peal of laughter. 'He's single, the right age—'

'And the very last man on earth I'd be interested in if I were looking for a man—which I'm not.'

Mardi's surprise was clear, then she nodded slowly. 'You're probably right. Michael's always been able to charm any woman he wants out of her knickers, but commitment's never been one of his strong points. "Love 'em and leave 'em" has always been his motto.'

Bethany wasn't surprised to hear it, and neither, she told herself firmly, did she need Mardi's warning. OK, so when Dr Harcus had smiled at her yesterday—before the rest of his visit had gone straight down the tubes—her heart had flipped over in a most disconcerting way, but handsome men didn't impress her any more.

They had once. When she'd first met Jake she'd been bowled over by his good looks and charm but, as she'd found out to her cost, when it came to stability and dependability she'd have been better off married to one of the seven dwarfs.

'Have we any cancellations today?' Mardi continued, reaching for the appointment book.

'Only your Uncle Bill at eleven o'clock. Apparently some emergency's come up.'

'Got cold feet, more like.' Her receptionist sniffed derisively. 'He'll be here at eleven o'clock, Bethany, or my name's not Mardi Muir.'

Bethany chuckled as she went through to her consulting room. Life would have been a lot easier if only all her patients had been related to her redoubtable receptionist. Life, a small voice pointed out at the back of her mind, would have been considerably easier if you'd listened to your mother and not dragged the children north to Orkney on a dream.

A deep sigh came from her as she sat down at her desk. Why, oh, why had she spoken to Michael Harcus the way she had yesterday? Antagonising him had been foolish, and making him look ridiculous had been downright crazy.

But he implied I was a mercenary quack, she argued.

And making him look stupid was a smart career move?

'Miss Linklater for you, Mrs Seton,' Mardi declared, popping her head round the consulting room door. 'Oh, and Bill Walker has rebooked his eleven o'clock appointment.'

A bubble of laughter sprang to Bethany's lips—a bubble she quickly suppressed as her receptionist ushered in a clearly very nervous Nora Linklater. Let Michael Harcus do his worst. With Mardi on her side she'd make a living somehow, and if the most arrogant, self-opinionated man she'd ever had the misfortune to meet believed she was simply going to give up on his say-so, he was very badly mistaken.

'How can I help you, Miss Linklater?' she asked when the woman sat down.

'I don't really know if you can,' she replied, her voice so low that Bethany had to lean across the desk to hear her. 'I'm going through the menopause, you see. Night sweats, hot flushes. Some days I seem to have no energy at all, and other days all I do is sit and…and…' Tears welled in her eyes, and she dug frantically into her pocket for a handkerchief. 'I'm sorry—so sorry…'

'Whatever for?' Bethany said gently. 'You're upset and quite understandably so. Now, I need a few personal details from you but, please, take your time. When was your last period?'

'Two years ago,' Miss Linklater replied, wiping her eyes. 'Just after my fifty-first birthday.'

'And your doctor is…?'

'Michael Harcus.'

Oh, great. That was all she needed today—yet another of Michael Harcus's patients consulting her. 'And have you spoken to Dr Harcus about your symptoms?'

'I went to see him a couple of months ago but all he offered me was psychiatric counselling.'

*Psychiatric counselling?* The arrogance of the man—the sheer unmitigated arrogance. Miss Linklater didn't need counselling. She needed someone to acknowledge her symptoms were real, not the implication that they were all in her mind.

'Are you taking any medication for any other condition, Miss Linklater?' Bethany asked, damping down her anger with difficulty.

The woman shook her head and, after checking her pulse, heart and lungs, Bethany launched into a series of questions about Miss Linklater's diet, work and lifestyle that clearly amazed her.

'I don't think I've ever been asked so many questions about myself before,' she said with a laugh when Bethany had finished.

'That's because herbal medicine takes a holistic approach to your health.' Bethany smiled. 'What I'm trying to do is to build up as complete a picture of you as I can before I prescribe anything.'

'And have you come to any decision?'

Bethany nodded. 'I think black cohosh would suit you. It's a herb with a very similar action to that of HRT—hormone replacement therapy—for controlling hot flushes, night sweats and flooding.'

'What about this bursting into tears I keep doing all the time?' Miss Linklater asked. 'I feel almost suicidal some days.'

If Michael Harcus were my doctor it wouldn't be suicide I'd be contemplating but murder, Bethany thought tersely. 'Lemon balm should help your mood swings, and St John's wort will also stop you feeling quite so depressed. If you could also add a little German chamomile or geranium diluted in some almond oil to your bath water every day, that should help, too.'

Miss Linklater looked dubious. 'It seems like an awful lot of things to take. Will it work?'

'Herbal medicines are much milder than synthetic ones so it might take a little while before we see any improvement,' Bethany admitted, 'but I promise you will. I'd like to see you again in a fortnight's time to find out how you're getting on,' she continued as Miss Linklater got to her feet, 'but if you have any worries in the meantime, please, don't hesitate to telephone me.'

'She looks a lot happier now than when she arrived,' Mardi observed after Bethany had shown Miss Linklater out.

'I'm not surprised,' Bethany replied tartly. 'Perhaps i
some doctors listened to their patients, instead of dismissing
their symptoms as psychosomatic, a lot more people migh
be happier!'

Mardi's eyebrows rose. 'Meaning any doctor in partic
ular, or just doctors in general?'

Professional discretion warred with anger inside
Bethany, and anger won. 'Michael Harcus.'

'Michael?' Mardi repeated in clear amazement. 'Are you
sure about this? Michael Harcus—'

'Is one of the best doctors you could ever hope to meet,
Anne Bichan finished with a smile as she appeared in the
office doorway. 'Not too early for my weekly massage, an
I?'

'Of course not,' Bethany replied, considerably flustered
at the thought of how much of her outburst Mrs Bichan
might have heard. But when the girl had slipped off he
blouse and climbed onto the massage table, she couldn'
prevent herself from saying, 'Anne, what you said abou
Dr Harcus. Did you mean it?'

'You bet.' Anne nodded as she turned over onto he
stomach and unhooked her bra. 'Working as a nurse in the
A and E department of Kirkwall Infirmary, I get to mee
all the local doctors and, believe me, some of them trea
nurses like dirt, but not Michael. In fact, he once told m
he thought nurses were more important than doctors be
cause it was their care that put patients back on the roa
to recovery.'

Bethany frowned. The man Nora Linklater had described
had sounded like an unsympathetic boor. The man she'
met herself hadn't exactly radiated goodwill and *bonhomie*
and yet Anne was saying he was wonderful.

Unconsciously she shook her head. Michael Harcus ha
come into her life less than twenty-four hours ago and ye
he never seemed to be out of her thoughts. Well, he coul
just take himself right out of her thoughts again, she de

cided as she mixed together the drops of sandalwood, palma rosa, and lemon she was going to use to ease the muscle strain in Anne Bichan's back.

She had a business to run, and two children to bring up, and Michael Harcus had no place in either concern. Let him look after his own patients, and she would take care of hers, and if their paths never ever crossed again she, for one, would be only too delighted.

'Since when did you become a closet masochist, Michael?' Connie asked, her lips curving as he took the glass of wine she was holding out to him.

'A closet...?'

'Didn't you say you'd rather have your toenails pulled out one by one than come to my barbecue? What happened? Pranged your dinghy, did you?'

'It's a yacht, Connie, as you very well know,' he replied tightly, 'and I'd be on it right now if I hadn't had to spend the whole damn day scouring Orkney for another mobile phone.'

Which didn't explain his presence here tonight, she decided. It didn't get dark even at midnight in Orkney in June so he could still have gone sailing, and yet he hadn't. Interesting. Very interesting. Perhaps she could encourage that interest a little more.

'Simon and I are really hoping Bethany can make it tonight,' she observed, waving airily to her husband who looked in serious need of help with the barbecue. 'She needs to get out more, and...' she slanted her brother a quick glance '...I was rather hoping to introduce her to Ralph Elliot.'

A burst of male laughter erupted from across the garden and Michael's eyebrows rose in distaste as he watched Ralph Elliot attempting to squirt some mayonnaise down the cleavage of one of the Lawrence girls. 'The man's a drunk, Connie.'

He cared who she introduced Bethany to? Now, that was even more interesting.

'Perhaps Ralph does drink a little too much at times,' she conceded. Lord, the accountant drank like a fish once he got started. 'But he can be quite amusing when he's sober, and he's rather good-looking, and—'

'When his long-suffering father dies he'll inherit one of Orkney's largest accountancy firms,' Michael finished for her dryly. 'It sounds like a match made in heaven. Let me know when you've arranged the wedding, Connie, and I'll be sure to keep the date free.'

His sister was about as subtle as a ten-ton truck, Michael thought as he strolled away, leaving her gazing in ill-concealed frustration after him. He couldn't have cared less if she'd told him she'd lined up Jack the Ripper for Bethany Seton. In fact, after a frustrating day spent trailing round the shops, he'd have been more than happy to have introduced Mrs Seton to Jack the Ripper personally.

Which didn't, of course, explain his presence here tonight, he realised, ignoring the tables and chairs Simon had placed round the garden and taking his glass of wine under the shade of the trees.

He'd come, he told himself, because by the time he'd got back from the shops it had been too late to go sailing. He'd come because Saturday night TV was always lousy. He'd come…

Oh, who the hell was he trying to kid? He'd come because he wanted to see Bethany Seton again. To find out if he'd imagined that disquieting flip of his heart. And when he turned and suddenly saw her, standing hesitantly by the side of the house, he realised to his dismay that he hadn't.

And then he noticed something else. Something no one else had seen, yet soon would, and before he had even rationalised his thoughts he was striding across the lawn to envelope her in a bear-like hug.

'D-Dr Harcus, what on earth are you doing?' she exclaimed, struggling vainly to escape from his grasp. Good grief, the man wasn't only an arrogant, obnoxious bully, he was a sex maniac as well. 'Let go of me at once!'

'Some of the buttons on the back of your dress are undone,' he muttered into her ear.

'Some of the...' She gazed up at him, open-mouthed, then crimson colour flooded her cheeks. 'Oh, my God, this is so embarrassing...'

'It won't be if you keep perfectly still and let me do them up for you.'

Let him do them up for her? Did he think she was stupid or something? After the way she'd treated him yesterday he'd probably undo a few more and really make her a laughing stock, but he must have read her mind because a slight smile curved his lips. 'Trust me.'

Trust him? No way—not ever. Trust a man whose reputation made Casanova look second rate? Trust a man she'd made to look ridiculous and who must be itching to pay her back? And yet, as his deep brown eyes held hers, she suddenly knew that she could. She didn't know how she knew it, she just did.

'OK,' she murmured, embarrassingly aware that everybody at the barbecue must be looking at them. 'But do you think you might let go of me a little before somebody decides we need a bucket of cold water thrown over us?'

A low, rumbling chuckle was his only response, but as his fingers began their slow descent down her spine she suddenly realised it wasn't just embarrassment she was feeling but something altogether more disturbing.

'Will you stand still?' he protested, as she shifted uncomfortably in his grasp.

Stand still? How could she stand still with her nose buried so deeply into his chest that she could feel his heart beating against her lips? How could she stand still when his fingers were creating such delicious sensations down

her spine—sensations she hadn't felt in years and didn't
want to feel now?

'Th-this would never have happened if I hadn't been in
such a hurry to get here t-tonight,' she stuttered, trying
desperately to divorce herself from the situation. 'My last
patient was late, you see, then Alistair started playing up—
saying he didn't need Mardi to babysit him because he
wasn't a baby any more—'

'All done.'

'S-sorry?'

'Your buttons—I've done them all up.'

She blinked. 'You have? But how…? I mean…'

A slow smile crept across his face. 'Call it a skill.'

That smile was dynamite. *He* was dynamite. Or at least
he would have been if she'd been a younger, more impres-
sionable woman. But she wasn't young any more, and marriage to Jake had swept away any susceptibility she might
once have had to a winning smile.

Quickly she extricated herself from his arms. 'Call it
practice more like,' she said wryly.

Which was as neat a way as any, he realised, of telling
him she knew all about his reputation.

'Mrs Seton—'

'Bethany, I'm so glad you made it!' Connie beamed,
hugging her friend enthusiastically while shooting her
brother a decidedly bemused glance. 'Now, I know I promised to introduce you to everyone but Simon's got in a bit
of a muddle with the barbecue so if Michael wouldn't mind
doing the honours…?'

She was gone before he could reply and, seeing
Michael's mouth slant into a rueful smile, Bethany said
hurriedly, 'Look, you don't need to babysit me. I'm perfectly capable of introducing myself.'

'I'm sure you are,' he observed, 'but I'd like to do it. I'd
also like to apologise for yesterday. I may have been a little
brusque.'

A *little* brusque? A *little*? An angry retort sprang to her lips and she crushed it down with difficulty.

'So you admit I would never tell George Abbot to stop taking his medication, and that my treatment might actually have helped him?' she said tightly.

'Yes, and no.'

'Yes, and—'

'Yes, I believe you didn't tell him to stop taking his medication, but I think his arthritis is probably in remission. It happens,' he continued, seeing her eyes flare, 'and, of course, there's the placebo effect—George thinking he's better simply because he's trying something new.'

Well, that was calling a spade a spade and no mistake, she decided grimly, but though she would have liked nothing better than to cut him down to size with a few well-chosen words she couldn't forget that he hadn't needed to come to her rescue over those dratted buttons.

'Perhaps I owe you an apology, too.' She was damned if she was going to be any more generous about it than he had been, but there was one thing she couldn't be niggardly over. 'About my buttons—'

'Forget it,' he interrupted dismissively. 'Perhaps you can do the same for me one day.'

The opportunity was too good to miss, and she didn't. 'You often wear dresses, do you, Dr Harcus?'

She had two dimples, he noticed, and at the moment both were dancing.

'The name's Michael, and I generally keep the frocks for the last Sunday in the month, and the blue chiffon suit for birthdays and weddings,' he said solemnly, and watched the laughter spread to her eyes. 'Which do you want first—introductions or food?'

'Food,' she said definitely. 'I'm starving.'

And she was, judging from the number of kebabs she heaped onto her plate.

'Sure you've got enough?' he couldn't resist saying as

he steered her towards the shady spot he'd found under the trees.

Guilt stained her cheeks. 'Should I only have taken one? I can take the others back—'

'I was only joking.' He laughed. 'It makes a change to see a woman with a healthy appetite.'

'Too healthy, I'm afraid.' She sighed as she sat down on the grass. 'I'm always promising myself I'll go on a diet tomorrow, and that's as far as it gets—promises.'

Her figure, he thought, was perfect. The boiler suit she'd worn yesterday had hinted at her feminine curves, but the green calf-length dress she was wearing tonight, with its fitted bodice and deep V-shaped neckline, accentuated every one of them. Accentuated and defined them to such a degree that he could feel an ache gathering in his groin— an ache as unwelcome as it was unexpected.

'Mrs Seton—'

'I think you've earned the right to call me Bethany, don't you?'

She was smiling—a smile that seemed to light up her whole face, illuminating it. Michael had seen a lot of beautiful women in his time—had dated quite a few of them, too—and Bethany Seton wasn't beautiful. And yet…

'Or you could stick with Mrs Seton if you prefer.'

He'd waited too long to reply. He could see it from the way the smile was fading from her lips, and he said quickly, 'I was just wondering what brought you to Orkney.' He hoped she'd buy the lie, and to his relief she did.

'According to my mother, it's because I need my head examined,' she said ruefully, and he laughed.

'No, seriously,' he pressed. 'Why did you come to Orkney?'

For a moment she said nothing, then her smile returned. 'Because I wanted to set up in business on my own, because I wanted a better life for my children. I saw a programme about Orkney on television and when Sorrel

Cottage was advertised for sale the very next day, it seemed…somehow it seemed like fate. I know that sounds silly,' she continued defensively as he shook his head at her, 'but I truly did feel it.'

'Wait until winter comes—or when the winds of the autumn equinox are so fierce you can hardly open your front door. It's beautiful now but Orkney summers are short.'

'I'll survive.'

'Not if you're planning on making your living as a herbalist, you won't.'

She put down the kebab she was eating. 'Is that a threat, Dr Harcus?'

There was a decided hint of steel in her voice and he shook his head. 'The name's Michael and, no, I'm not threatening you. Just warning you that Orcadians are notoriously slow at accepting anything new.'

'But herbalism isn't new,' she protested. 'Eighty per cent of the world's population relies solely on herbs for their health.'

'Only because there's no alternative.'

'Rubbish! People use herbs because they *work*. Look at St John's wort. Even *The Lancet* admitted it could treat depression just as effectively as synthetic antidepressants but without the side effects of pharmaceutically created drugs.'

'Bethany—'

'And meadowsweet is every bit as good as aspirin for treating aches and pains but it doesn't cause internal bleeding in people with sensitive stomachs.'

'Bethany—'

'And ginkgo—'

'OK, OK,' he interrupted, holding up his hands in a gesture of surrender. 'You can get off your soapbox now.'

'But you're still not convinced,' she said shrewdly. 'Look, I would never dream of saying no one should ever have surgery or take synthetic pills. Good grief, my own

son is a diabetic and I'd never tell him not to take h
insulin. All I'm saying is that herbalism has a place in th
twenty-first century.'

Not if it meant that people like Amy Wylie died need
lessly, he thought. Not if people chose quack remedies ove
orthodox medicine and suffered agonising deaths whe
they could have been cured.

He cleared his throat. 'I'd be a fool not to see the valu
of massage for certain conditions, or to appreciate that act
puncture and osteopathy have their uses for muscle an
joint disorders, but herbalism, Bethany…' He shook h
head. 'It belongs in the Dark Ages, and that's where
should stay.'

'Even though without it we would never have had dig
talis, found naturally in foxgloves and manufactured as d
goxin for cardiac drugs to treat heart disorders?' she de
clared, stretching past him to pick up a napkin to wipe he
fingers. 'Or quinine to treat malaria from the bark of th
cinchona tree, or cocaine from the leaves of the coca plan
to ease pain in cancer sufferers?'

He could have given her a long list of drugs that coul
only have been developed by pharmaceutical companie:
but he didn't. He was too busy wondering how his bod
could possibly have gone from near dormancy to screamin
awareness in the space of half an hour.

And it was a screaming awareness. Just the touch of he
arm against his chest as she'd reached for the napkin ha
sent his heart rate into overdrive.

He didn't want to sit on the grass discussing the pro
and cons of herbal medicine with Bethany Seton. What h
wanted was to take her in his arms, pull her hair free fron
that damned French pleat and discover if her lips tasted a
sweet as they looked. What he really wanted, he realise
as he stared across at her and felt his groin tighten, was t
find out if the tantalising curves he could see—and had hel
all too briefly—were real or the result of clever underwea

'Don't tell me you've thrown in the towel already, Michael?'

There was laughter in her eyes. Laughter that showed she didn't have a clue—thank God—of the thoughts that were sending a slow crawl of heat up the back of his neck.

'I think I should start introducing you to everyone,' he said, abruptly getting to his feet.

'Chicken!' she mocked.

Idiot more like, he decided ruefully as he kept as far away from her as possible for the rest of the evening, only to find his eyes constantly searching for her.

Why the hell was he avoiding a woman he found attractive? He was single, Bethany was single, so why shouldn't they enjoy one another, then go their separate ways? It wouldn't hurt anybody—it wouldn't harm anybody. The only person hurting right now was himself, and for what? A stupid pledge he'd made two years ago when Sarah had walked out on him.

Well, two years was a long time to remain celibate, he thought when he saw Bethany making her farewells. Two years was too long, he decided as he followed her.

'Do you know anything about cars?' she asked when he caught up with her beside her ancient Vauxhall. 'Mine won't start, and I don't know why.'

'Have you got any petrol in it?'

'Oh, very funny.' She grimaced. 'Yes, it's got petrol and, no, my battery's not flat. The engine just won't start.'

He lifted the bonnet, poked around for a while, then shook his head. 'You've got a cracked distributor cap. Unless you want a hefty Saturday night call-out charge, my advice is to leave your car here and call the garage tomorrow morning.'

And it would be a hefty call-out charge, she realised. Eric Foubister might be Mardi's fiancé but he didn't run a charity.

'I'll drive you home,' Michael continued, clearly reading her mind.

'I can't ask you to do that,' she protested.

'You didn't.' He smiled. 'I offered.'

Which meant that he'd rescued her twice in one evening, she realised as they drove out of Kirkwall towards Evie. Twice he'd helped her without being asked, and yet yesterday… Yesterday he'd behaved with all the sensitivity of an arrogant, obnoxious bully.

It didn't make any sense. *He* didn't make any sense. Either she and Nora Linklater had both caught him on a bad day, or he was the original Dr Jekyll and Mr Hyde, and he didn't look like a monster.

Maybe she should ask him about Miss Linklater? And then again, perhaps not, she decided as she glanced quickly across at him, then away again. Some things were best forgotten. Things like the hefty garage bill she was undoubtedly going to get, she thought with a deep sigh.

'Penny for them?'

His eyes were on her, thoughtful, pensive, and she managed to smile. 'I'd be robbing you if I charged anything. Would you like to come in for a coffee before you drive back to Kirkwall?' she added, noticing they'd almost reached Sorrel Cottage.

He nodded but he wasn't one bit deceived by that smile. 'Bethany, if there's something wrong—something I can help you with…'

'Of course there isn't,' she protested. 'What could possibly be wrong on such a lovely evening?'

In other words, mind your own business, he thought, smiling inwardly, but he didn't intend to. He intended to make Bethany Seton very much his business from now on.

And his intention lasted until Mardi had gone, her eyes sparkling with keen interest at his presence, and Bethany had ushered him into the sitting room with instructions to make himself comfortable while she made the coffee. It asted until his eyes fell on the toys and books scattered round the floor, on the half-finished little girl's dress draped over the sewing machine, and he found himself wondering how on earth he could ever have told himself that Bethany Seton was single.

She wasn't single. She was a divorced mother of two who'd been badly hurt by somebody in the past, and the last thing she needed was a man like him in her life—a man who was only comfortable with brief affairs. She needed somebody to take care of her, somebody to be there for her, and so did the two children who stared innocently out from the photograph on the mantelpiece.

Bethany Seton wasn't the kind of woman to be picked up, enjoyed and then discarded. She deserved better than that—much better than that—and the best thing he could do for her—the only thing—was to keep as far away from her as possible.

'I'm afraid I'll have to take a rain check on that coffee,' he said the minute she appeared, carrying two cups. 'I'm on call tonight, you see,' he added as she gazed at him in surprise, 'and my bleeper's just gone off.'

'It's nothing serious, I hope?' she said, instantly concerned.

He shook his head, feeling like a louse for lying to her but knowing he had to leave, get away.

'I can't thank you enough for driving me home,' she continued as she accompanied him to the front door. 'It was very kind of you.'

Kindness had nothing to do with it, as he very well knew, but he forced himself to smile. 'It's what friends are for, Bethany.'

'Are we friends?' she asked, looking up at him a little uncertainly. 'I hope we can be, but after yesterday…'

'Forget about yesterday.' He reached out and clasped one of her hands in his. 'I should like…I would very much like to be your friend, Bethany Seton.'

And she'd like to be his, she thought as she watched him drive away. A husband she could do without, a boyfriend she didn't need, but someone to talk to, to laugh with... She put her hand to her cheek absently. It was still warm from the touch of his fingers and unconsciously her lips curved into a smile. Yes, she could do with a friend.

# CHAPTER THREE

'THE headache's on the left side of your head, you said?' Michael declared as he peered through his ophthalmoscope into William Oliver's eyes, looking for any sign of intra-cranial pressure which might indicate bleeding or a tumour.

'That's right, Doctor. I'm not a weakling but I've never experienced pain like it. My wife wondered—'

'Any weakness in your arms and legs?' Michael inter-rupted. 'Stiff neck or fever?'

'None at all.'

Nor was there any sign of intracranial pressure that Michael could see.

'Do you suffer from migraines at all, William?' he asked, straightening up and staring at the left side of the pen-sioner's face to see if there were any signs of drooping, which could suggest the man had suffered a minor stroke.

'Never had any kind of headache at all until I got this one, Doctor.'

Michael frowned. In the absence of a stiff neck or fever, he could safely rule out the possibility of meningitis, and nervous tension often caused excruciatingly painful head-aches, and yet, and yet...

'Have you fallen recently, William?'

'Look, Doctor, I might be sixty-five but I'm not dod-dery—'

'Just asking, OK?' Michael broke in with a smile as William glared at him. 'You said you've had this headache for a week?'

'I didn't really want to bother you with it, Doctor, so I went to see Mrs Seton—'

'Bethany?' Michael exclaimed without thinking, only to

41

flush slightly as William's eyebrows rose. 'And what did Mrs Seton say?'

'That I ought to come and see you.'

So she hadn't been lying when she'd said she always sent patients to their own doctor if something worried her.

'I'll like you to have a CAT scan, William,' he declared quickly extracting a sheet of paper from his desk.

'A CAT scan?'

'Computerised axial tomographic scanning, to give it its full title. It's simply a very sophisticated combination of a computer and X-ray machine which can take pictures of your brain and body at different angles,' Michael continued with a reassuring smile as the pensioner gazed at him in alarm. 'It doesn't hurt and you'll be in and out of the hospital in half an hour.'

'Yes, but—'

'It's only a precaution, William. I'm sure there's absolutely nothing for you to worry about.'

He prayed there wasn't as he showed the pensioner out, he was almost sure there wasn't, but he couldn't rid himself of the niggling feeling that there was.

'What on earth did you say to Mr Oliver?' Simon asked when he joined him in his consulting room for a post-surgery discussion. 'He looked absolutely terrified out of his wits when he left.'

'I'm sending him for a CAT scan. He's had a severe headache for a week and it could simply be due to nervous tension, but I'd like to be sure.'

Simon nodded. 'I noticed Linda Balfour in the waiting room earlier. She's not looking any better, is she?'

Michael cradled his coffee in his hands and leant back wearily in his seat. 'The trouble with chronic fatigue syndrome—or ME, as the newspapers will persist in erroneously calling it—is that there's so little we can do for the condition, apart from offering vitamin supplements and antidepressants.'

'I wonder...' Simon paused and cleared his throat. 'I wonder if Bethany could do anything to help her? Massage wouldn't do Linda any harm, Michael,' he continued quickly, seeing his brother-in-law's eyebrows snap together, 'and I read an article recently about a group of German doctors who reported quite encouraging results after treating CFS sufferers with a herb called echinacea.'

'No.'

'But—'

'Forget it, Simon.'

'Michael, this isn't like you.' And neither was the distinctly daunting look Simon was receiving from his brother-in-law, but he ploughed on nevertheless. 'You've always been open to new ideas. In fact, you were the first doctor I ever knew to send a patient to an acupuncturist.'

'Bethany's a herbalist, not an acupuncturist.'

'And I think she could be useful to us. I'm not saying we should embrace *all* of her ideas—God forbid—but I've been thinking that it might not be a bad idea to ask her if she'd like to become affiliated with the practice—have rooms here.'

'*What?*' Michael exclaimed, sitting bolt upright in his seat and sending the remains of his coffee splattering over his desk in the process. 'Good God, where on earth did you come up with that crackpot idea? Or maybe you didn't,' he continued, his eyes narrowing. 'It was Connie, wasn't it?'

A betraying flush of colour crept over Simon's cheeks. 'She might have mentioned it—in passing, as it were.'

'In a pig's eye it was in passing,' Michael declared grimly, pulling some tissues out of the box on his desk and attacking the spilt coffee. 'And was it also her idea to send Linda Balfour to Bethany?'

'Of course it wasn't, but asking Bethany to join us... Michael, is it really so crazy?'

It was insane, he thought with horror. Not only would it send out all the wrong signals to their patients—indicating

their approval for a profession he considered at best mis-
guided and at worst sheer chicanery—but he'd be forced to
see Bethany every day. Be near her every day. And he'd
just spent the last two weeks trying not to think about her.

'Michael…?'

His brother-in-law was staring at him uncertainly and he
sighed. Unlike Simon, he didn't have to live with Connie.
Unlike Simon, he could be as rude to his sister as he
wanted, then go home and close his own front door.

'I'll think about it,' he lied, and saw clear relief appear
in Simon's eyes—relief that very quickly turned to concern
when Michael winced as he leant forward to pick up the
stack of patient case files on his desk.

'Michael, that shoulder of yours doesn't seem to be getting any better.'

'It's only a strained muscle,' he replied dismissively,
leading the way out of his consulting room. 'I'll live.'

'Connie says it's your just desserts for going sailing instead of coming to our Saturday barbecues.' Simon grinned.

Connie would say that, Michael thought as he handed
his files with a smile to Rose at Reception, but wild horses
wouldn't have dragged him to another of his sister's barbecues—not when there was even the remotest chance that
Bethany might be there, too.

Which doesn't mean you should refuse even to consider
sending Linda Balfour to see her, a little voice in the back
of his mind pointed out as he left the Harbour Medical
Centre.

Herbalism, smerbalism. He snorted as he got into his car.
The cures people spoke of were undoubtedly all wishful
thinking anyway.

And if they weren't—if Bethany really could do something to help?

He frowned as he stared out at the sparkling waters of
Kirkwall Bay. The massage would definitely help Linda to
relax, and as for the echinacea… He'd read the same article

as Simon and the results certainly sounded impressive. And
Bethany could do with the money if the word on the grapevine about her lack of patients was correct.

Well, what the hell did she expect? he thought, thrusting
his hands angrily through his hair. He'd warned her that
people would be wary of trying anything new, and if she
was in trouble financially it was her own fault. Dragging
her children north to Orkney on the strength of a dream
had just been plain stupid.

And yet, as he continued to stare out at the white-crested
waves, he found himself remembering how tired she'd
looked when he'd driven her home—tired, and just a little
defeated. Eyes as beautiful as hers shouldn't have dark
shadows under them. Eyes as gentle as hers were made for
laughter, not worry.

He sighed as he started his car. It would do no harm to
talk to her about Linda Balfour. He had the afternoon free
until evening surgery and talking cost nothing, committed
him to nothing. And if Bethany intended staying on in
Orkney he could hardly avoid her for ever. Perhaps it was
time to face her again, to rid himself once and for all of
the disturbing thoughts that plagued him.

But it wasn't disturbing thoughts that assailed him when
he arrived at Sorrel Cottage and saw her digging in the
garden. It was anger.

'What the hell do you think you're doing?' he demanded,
seeing her straighten up with an effort as he got out of his
car. 'That ground hasn't been dug over for years!'

'Now he tells me,' she replied, her eyes dancing.

'I'm being serious, Bethany,' he protested. 'You should
have got a man in to do that.'

'Can't afford one,' she said simply. 'Are you just passing, or have you time for a chat and a glass of orange
juice?'

Michael fought to contain his anger. 'I wanted to talk to
you about a patient of mine, but I'll take the drink if it'll

make you put down that damn spade before you hospitalise yourself!'

'Rubbish.' She laughed. 'I'm a lot stronger than I look. I have to be or I'd never be able to do whole body massages.'

She massaged people all over? She massaged *men* all over, including their... He swallowed, hard. 'So why aren't you doing that, instead of spending one of the hottest afternoons in July half killing yourself?'

'Tuesdays are always quiet,' she said defensively. And Wednesdays, and Thursdays, and Fridays, but she had no intention of telling him that. 'Do you mind if we have our drinks out here?' she said instead, putting down the spade and absently wiping her hands on her T-shirt. 'Not only do I have the most beautiful view in the world, with Eynhallow Sound and the hills of Rousay beyond, it's a lot cooler out here than it is indoors.'

'Outside sounds great.' And a cold drink sounded even better, he decided, trying desperately not to notice that her simple action had pressed her damp T-shirt even closer to her full breasts. 'Do you...? Would you like any help?'

She shook her head, then gazed at him with slight concern. 'Are you OK? I can bring you some chamomile tea instead of orange juice if this heat is bothering you?'

The only heat bothering him at the moment was the heat emanating from a region of his anatomy he thought chamomile tea unlikely to alleviate. 'Orange juice will be fine.'

She nodded, but as she went into the house he couldn't prevent a wry grin from curving his lips as he slipped off his jacket. It was quite obvious she didn't have the faintest idea of the effect she had on him, whereas he... He'd never considered himself a vain man, but seeing Bethany again was as sure as heck proving to be an ego-deflating experience.

'I know you, don't I?'

He glanced round with a start, then adjusted his gaze downwards.

'You're Dr Harcus—the doctor from Kirkwall,' Katie continued, hopping from one foot to the other, her auburn curls bouncing as she gazed up at him. 'Have you come to see Mummy?'

He nodded. 'Your mother's—'

'I wanted to play with Alistair but he told me to go away and bother somebody else.' Her small face set into a scowl. 'Boys are a pain.'

Michael buried his amusement. 'I guess we can all be a bit of a pain at times.'

'I've got new sandals.' Katie held out a foot for his inspection. 'I really wanted red ones, but they didn't have any in the shop. Have you got a daddy?'

'Have I...?'

'I haven't,' she continued conversationally before he could pull his scattered wits together. 'Well, I do really, but he doesn't live with us any more, and I haven't seen him for ages and ages.'

What in the world was he supposed to say to that? he wondered in dismay. He had so little experience of kids. Hell, he had *no* experience of kids, apart from asking them to 'open wide' or 'take a deep breath'. 'Katie—'

'She's not supposed to talk to strangers.'

Michael turned to see Alistair watching them, his face hostile, challenging. 'I'm hardly a stranger, Alistair,' he said gently. 'In fact, I was rather hoping we might all become friends.'

That the prospect wasn't high on Alistair's list of 'must haves' was clear. 'Mum said you were to have your snack at three,' he declared, turning to his sister. 'It's way past that now.'

'Are you staying long?' Katie asked, ignoring her brother's comment, her large grey eyes fixed on Michael.

'A little while, I think,' he said with a nod.

'Good.' She beamed, skipping off towards the house. 'Because I like you.'

Michael chuckled as he watched her go, but his amusement disappeared when he noticed that Alistair was still staring at him, his chin now set into a decidedly mutinous line.

'Alistair—'

'I heard Katie telling you about Dad. He took off years ago but we don't miss him. We get along just fine—me, Mum and Katie.'

'I'm sure you do—'

'Mum doesn't need any more hassle.' The boy's chin wobbled for a second, then he brought it back under rigid control. 'She's had enough in the past.'

Was he being warned off? It sounded very much as though he was and, though Michael supposed he should have found it funny, there was something touching about the way the ten-year-old was trying to protect his mother. Something that brought an unaccustomed lump to his throat. 'Alistair, listen—'

'*There* you are,' Bethany said with relief as she came out of the house and saw her son. 'You remember Dr Harcus, don't you?'

'I remember him.'

Her son's tone, and the look which accompanied it, were just one shade shy of downright insolence, and a flush of embarrassed colour appeared on Bethany's cheeks.

'I was getting ready to send out a search party for you,' she declared, putting down the tray she was carrying and pulling over two of the oldest-looking deckchairs Michael had ever seen. 'You know how important it is for you to eat regularly because of your diabetes—'

'I should do. You never stop telling me.'

The colour on Bethany's cheeks deepened. 'Alistair—'

'Can I go now?' he demanded. 'I've some reading I want to catch up on.'

And before Bethany could reply, he had taken to his heels and banged into the house.

For a second Bethany said nothing, then she cleared her throat awkwardly. 'I'm sorry about that. Alistair... He used to be such a friendly, sociable little boy, but these past two years... In fact, ever since we discovered he was a diabetic, he seems to want to be on his own all the time.'

'Maybe he feels uncomfortable with his condition—feels it marks him out from the rest of the crowd,' Michael observed, taking the glass of orange juice she was holding out to him and sitting down on one of the deckchairs, praying it would take his weight. 'Or maybe he just likes his own company. Lots of people do.'

'I guess so,' she murmured, clearly unconvinced, 'but I'd hoped the move here might change him, make him more sociable again.'

'He doesn't like Orkney?'

'He loves it, but all the things he's interested in—bird-watching, reading, archaeology—they're all hobbies you can do on your own.'

'Bethany—'

'I'm boring you rigid, talking about my family, aren't I?' she said with a smile that didn't reach her eyes.

'Of course you're not. Alistair—'

'Probably just likes his own company, as you said. Now, who's this patient you wanted to talk to me about?'

It wasn't a very subtle way of changing the conversation—in fact, it wasn't subtle at all—but he could tell by the set of her jaw—so very like her son's if she did but know it—that he'd get nowhere at the moment if he pressed her.

'You believe CFS actually exists, then?' she declared after he'd told her about Linda Balfour. 'A lot of doctors dismiss it as psychological.'

'I think both mind and body are probably involved. From what I've read, Linda has the classic chronic fatigue syndrome personality—a hardworking perfectionist who finds it hard to relax and is inclined to become depressed and introverted.'

'A description which could probably fit half the population and yet they don't all become CFS sufferers,' Bethany observed. 'Why come to me? I thought you didn't approve of herbalism?'

He smiled. 'I don't, but nothing I'm doing seems to be helping.'

'Well, that's honest enough.' She laughed. 'OK, if she were my patient I'd give her twice weekly massages to help her relax and to increase the number of T cells produced by her immune system.'

'You know about T cells?' he said in surprise.

Her eyebrows rose in what he could only describe as an old-fashioned look. 'The bone marrow, thymus gland, spleen and lymph glands are the major elements of the immune system. They produce several types of white blood cells which produce antibodies to neutralise dangerous organisms at the prompting of other cells—called helper T cells—and then stop producing antibodies when the suppressor T cells signal them to do so.'

'OK, you do kno—'

'If you're in good health the helper and suppressor T cells are in balance,' she continued inexorably, 'so antibodies are produced only when needed. If something goes wrong, and the suppressor cells dominate, the system can become weakened or immunodeficient. Conversely, if the helper T cells dominate, then the immune system becomes overactive and starts attacking body tissues, which is what happens in multiple sclerosis.'

'That was a very stupid question, wasn't it?' He grinned.

She shrugged. 'I read a lot.'

'So what herbs would you give Linda?'

'Liquorice and ginseng to support her adrenal glands, skullcap to support the nervous system, and gingko to improve any impaired circulation in the brain. Is she on anti-depressants?'

He nodded. 'She is, and I'm not very happy about it.'

'St John's wort could be useful, then. It's a very effective mood-enhancer and antidepressant. The main thing I'd give her, however, is echinacea. It's a herb—'

'Native Americans used to stimulate the immune system, and to prevent infections by increasing the flow of white blood cells.' His eyes sparkled wickedly as she stared at him, open-mouthed. 'I read a lot, too.'

She chuckled, then grew serious. 'Look, I think I can help her, but the real question is—do you want me to?'

He sighed. 'To be honest with you, I don't know. If you could give me good scientific evidence that herbalism really works…'

'How can I do that when so few hospitals will allow herbalists in to test their remedies?' she protested. 'And do you honestly think any drug company is ever going to put money into trials which might prove that a herb which can be easily and cheaply acquired is able to do the job just as well as a product they've made millions out of? The only way I can give you evidence, Michael, is if someone does proper research, and it's not going to happen.'

She was right—it wasn't, and yet…

'Bethany, I'm a man of science, and you're asking me to forget everything I've ever been taught.'

'I'm not—believe me, I'm not,' she insisted. 'In fact, if I ever needed an operation I'd be on your doorstep in a minute. All I want is for people like you, trained in conventional medicine, to accept that you don't have a monopoly on healing, and that you can learn something from other branches of the profession.'

It didn't seem an unreasonable request but he couldn't make a decision right away. OK, so Bethany's qualifications in herbalism sounded impressive, but Linda Balfour's health was at stake here, as well as his own professional reputation, and if anything went wrong…

'Let me think about it, OK?' he said, getting to his feet.

'What happened to your shoulder?' she asked, seeing him wince as he eased himself into his jacket.

He shrugged and wished he hadn't. 'I pulled a muscle a couple of weeks ago. It's one of the hazards of being a weekend sailor, I'm afraid. I'm not as fit as I should be.'

He looked pretty fit from where she was standing, but she didn't say that.

'I could try massaging it if you like,' she said instead.

He grinned. 'Touting for business, Bethany, or trying to score a professional point? I'm sorry but I don't have time today.'

'It won't take any time at all if you don't mind me massaging you dressed like this. Oh, come on, Michael, what harm can it do?' she continued, sensing his indecision. 'Being in pain all the time can't exactly be the best advertisement for your medical skills, can it?'

She was right, and he sighed. 'OK, you've sold it to me.'

Quickly she led the way into the house, but as he followed her down the corridor, carefully negotiating the usual haphazard conglomeration of abandoned toys, a STRICTLY No ADMITTANCE notice pinned to one of the doors caught his eye. 'What's in there?'

'My dispensary. People can't exactly drop into their local chemist for the things I prescribe, can they, Michael?' she added with a chuckle as he gazed at her in surprise. 'Want to take a look?'

'Why not?' He smiled, but when she unlocked the door and ushered him into a room hung with bunches of herbs and redolent with the pungent aromas of spices, his jaw dropped. 'Good grief. ''Eye of newt and toe of frog…'''

'''Wool of bat, and tongue of dog,''' she said laughingly. '*Macbeth*, right? So, which of the three witches am I?'

'I'll let you know when I decide,' he said with a grin. 'Did you dry all these plants yourself?' he continued, fascinated in spite of himself.

'Not the more exotic ones. I have a contact in London who's very good at tracing herbs that can only be found abroad.'

'What's this?' he asked, reaching up to touch what looked like dried slivers of wood.

'Yohimbine. It's the bark of a West African tree traditionally used as a male aphrodisiac but more commonly used now as a cure for impotence.'

He released the bark as though he'd been stung, and she was amused to see a tide of dark colour sweep across his cheeks. So Michael Harcus was shy about that sort of thing, was he? Now, that was a surprise.

'Are there any illnesses you can't—or won't—treat?' he asked, hurrying to the door.

'Oh, heavens, lots,' she replied, following him. 'Chest pain if it's accompanied by acute pain in the chest, arms or throat. Unexplained dizziness, coughing up blood, inexplicable weight loss and fatigue, changes in shape and size of mole, passing blood—'

'OK, OK, I get the picture.' He laughed.

'Herbalism works best when treating long-term and recurring disorders,' she continued as she locked the dispensary door again. 'Migraine, arthritis, respiratory and circulatory problems. Things like that.'

'I see,' he murmured, nodding to Mardi who had popped her head round the office door and was gazing at him with keen interest. 'You'll be wanting my jacket off for this massage, I suppose?' he continued, easing it from his shoulders as he followed Bethany into her consulting room.

'What I want is for you to answer a few questions first about your medical history, lifestyle and general state of health, including any current medication,' she replied, sitting down behind her desk and reaching for her notebook.

'Sickeningly good health both now and in the past, apart from this shoulder, and no current medication.'

'Lifestyle?'

'Don't smoke, drink only in moderation.'

'Nightclubs, discos?'

His eyebrows rose. 'In Orkney?'

She laughed. 'What about stress?'

His eyebrows climbed even higher. 'Bethany, I'm a doctor.'

'OK, lots of stress. Any injuries in the past, or surgery that may have contributed to your condition?'

He shook his head and she leant back in her seat. 'OK. Could you walk across the room for me?'

'Could I...? What on earth for?' he asked in confusion.

'I need to see how you walk.'

'With one foot in front of the other like everybody else.'

'Michael—'

'OK, OK,' he said with a sigh, getting to his feet. Slowly he walked across the room, then back again. 'What now? Press-ups, headstands?'

'What I want is for you to stop complaining, get behind that screen and take your clothes off.'

'Take my clothes off?' he repeated, hoping against hope that he might have misheard her, but with a sinking feeling knowing that he hadn't.

'I'm not exactly going to be able to give you much of a massage if you keep them on, am I?' she exclaimed.

'Look, perhaps we should do this some other time,' he said quickly, feeling a betraying blush of colour sweeping across his cheeks. Hell, he hadn't blushed since he was fifteen when his mother had caught him necking with the girl next door. 'I've evening surgery tonight—'

'Why, Dr Harcus, I do believe you're *shy*,' Bethany interrupted, with a gurgle of laughter. 'Look, I've seen all shapes and sizes in my work, and it's not as though you're going to be naked. Most of you will be covered with a towel.'

'Yes, but—'

'Michael, this is crazy. You're in pain and I can help you. Surely it's worth losing a little bit of your dignity to have your shoulder helped?'

It wasn't his dignity he was afraid of losing but he could hardly tell her that, and reluctantly he went behind the screen and began peeling off his clothes.

'What witch's brew is that you're concocting?' he asked, as an exotic aroma drifted across the top of the screen towards him.

'Just ginger, chamomile and a little nutmeg in some avocado oil.'

'Bethany, I've got evening surgery at six,' he protested. 'I can't arrive there smelling like an Arabian brothel.'

'And what, pray, tell, does Dr Harcus know of Arabian brothels?' she asked, her dimples dancing.

'Bethany—'

'Michael, it's a well-established fact that massaging with oils from aromatic plants works considerably better than just using plain oil.'

'Yes, but—'

'And any smell will evaporate really quickly. Now, are you ready?'

As he'd ever be, he thought, edging awkwardly out from behind the screen and swiftly lying face down on the massage table.

'The massage system I use is based on Swedish massage techniques,' she declared, clucking in irritation as she noticed he'd pulled his towel up as far round his shoulders as it could go. 'The first step is effleurage—it's a gentle stroking action to aid circulation and relax tense muscles.'

'Is it?' he muttered, shifting uncomfortably on the table as she pulled the towel down to his waist and began sliding her hands smoothly and rhythmically over his shoulders in wide fanning strokes. Normally he had a lot of admiration for the Swedes, but if they thought this was relaxing they needed their heads examined.

'Aromatherapists believe that by massaging this way the oil molecules are absorbed into the bloodstream and the nervous system,' she continued. 'The massage also stimulates the lymphatic system, which helps to remove metabolic wastes from the body. Once you're sufficiently relaxed I can begin petrissage—or kneading—which stretches and relaxes muscles.'

'And…um…how…how long does a typical massage last?'

'Oh, about an hour usually for a full body massage— around forty minutes for your back and shoulders.'

She could have sworn he muttered, 'God almighty.' But if he was still feeling embarrassed at having to strip off, he certainly had no need to be.

In fact, she thought he had the most beautiful shoulders she'd ever seen. Broad and muscular, and golden brown. His arms were brown, too, as were his thighs and legs. He must wear only shorts when he was sailing. Or maybe he didn't wear anything at all with nobody to see him. Maybe he was actually that glorious golden brown colour all over. Her eyes drifted of their own accord to where the towel was just covering his buttocks. It would be easy enough to find out…

Ye gods, what in the world was she thinking? she wondered, feeling a wash of hot colour sweep across her cheeks. He was a patient. You didn't regard a patient as a person when you were massaging them. You saw them simply as a malfunctioning body you could help. But, boy, oh, boy, did he have some body!

'A lot of people tell me this makes them feel very sleepy,' she forced herself to comment as she began applying circular pressure to the back of his neck.

Personally Michael thought he'd never felt more wide

awake in his life. Thank God for the towel—thank God he was lying on his stomach—because if he hadn't been, there would have been two extremely embarrassed people in Bethany's consulting room.

'Am I hurting you?' she asked, feeling him tense under her fingers.

'A…a little.'

He sounded slightly strangled, and she gazed down at him with concern. This wasn't supposed to hurt. It was supposed to be relaxing, comforting.

Deliberately she lightened her touch until it was no more than a feather-light caress across his back and shoulders, and heard a muffled groan.

'Look, this shouldn't be hurting you,' she said quickly. 'Maybe the problem's in your chest. If you could turn over for me I could try some frottage—'

'Not on your life,' he gasped, and before she could answer he had shot off the table, dragging his towel behind him, and disappeared behind the screen.

'Michael—'

'I'm afraid I'll have to leave the rest of the massage for another day.' His voice sounded tense, strained.

'But I've only just started—'

'That's the trouble,' he muttered.

'Sorry?' she said in confusion.

'I— Look, I haven't got time for this today,' he declared, emerging from behind the screen having dressed in record time. 'I've surgery at six, and I've still got to get back to Kirkwall.'

'Can I make you an appointment for when you've got more time?' she said, having almost to run to keep up with him as he headed out the door and down the corridor. 'I'm worried about that shoulder. If it's giving you so much pain—'

'It's fine.'

'Michael—'

'Thanks for the drink.'

'You're welcome, but, Michael—' She was talking to thin air.

With a wave of his hand, he got into his car and drove off at speed, and a deep frown pleated her forehead as she closed the door and walked slowly along the corridor. What in the world had she done to make him race off like that? OK, her massage seemed to have hurt him rather more than she'd expected, but he hadn't given her enough time to get to the root of the problem.

'Michael left in a bit of a hurry, didn't he?'

Her receptionist was leaning against the office door, watching her, and she nodded. 'He has a surgery tonight at six.'

Mardi glanced down at her watch. 'And it'll take him an hour and a half to drive to Kirkwall?' She shook her head. 'What on earth did you do to the poor man?'

'I was giving him a massage—'

'Ah.'

'And what's that supposed to mean?' Bethany demanded.

'Oh, come on, Bethany.' Mardi chuckled. 'The touch of your dainty digits on his body, the feel of your hands caressing him…'

'Get out of here!' Bethany exclaimed with a peal of laughter. 'He's a friend, Mardi, that's all.'

'So all that laughing I heard in the garden earlier didn't mean anything?'

Bethany rolled her eyes heavenwards with exasperation. 'It is possible, you know, to talk to a man, laugh with him, and remain just friends.'

'Maybe if the man is fat, bald and fifty,' her receptionist observed, 'but Michael Harcus? My God, the man simply oozes sex appeal.'

'Not in my direction, he doesn't,' Bethany declared, trying very hard not to remember her reaction when she'd seen hose brown shoulders. 'I don't even think of him as a man, nd I'm damn sure he doesn't think of me as a woman. We're *friends*.'

'Yea, right.' Mardi grinned as she went back into her office. 'Just watch your step, OK?'

Bethany opened her mouth, closed it again, considered following her receptionist into the office to continue the argument, then dismissed the idea.

Watch her step, indeed! Good grief, Michael Harcus would never be interested in her in a million years. Interested in a fat, ordinary-looking woman of thirty-three with two children and stretch marks? A woman who couldn't remember the last time she'd been to a hair-dresser's far less when she'd put on any make-up? No way, not ever.

And that was exactly what she wanted, she told herself as she caught sight of her reflection in the hall mirror and unaccountably found herself wishing she were taller, slimmer, younger. It had taken her five years to get her life together after Jake had left, and the last thing she needed was some man disturbing her peace of mind.

Plain friendship was better, simpler and safer all round. And friendship, she reminded herself very firmly as she stuck out her tongue belligerently at her reflection, was all she wanted.

# CHAPTER FOUR

'YOU know what's wrong with you, don't you?' Conni
observed as Bethany carried their empty coffee-cups acros
to the sink. 'You've got a bad attack of the blues.'

Bethany ran some water into the sink and sighed.
know, and the ridiculous thing is I don't even know why
My business is picking up, the children are fine, but...' Sh
shook her head impatiently. 'What I need is to stop feelin
sorry for myself.'

And to start counting my blessings, she decided as sh
glanced out of the kitchen window and saw her son in th
garden.

Ever since Alistair had discovered there was nothin
Michael didn't know about the history of Orkney, he'
been a different boy. He could still be moody, of course
and he still spent far too much time on his own, but Michae
was gradually coaxing him out of his shell and she thanke
heaven for it.

'Mardi... Mardi told me Michael's become quite a reg
ular visitor over the last month,' Connie commented, pick
ing her words with care.

'And how.' Bethany chuckled. 'I'm treating one of hi
patients, you see, and I think he's secretly terrified I'
going to poison her!'

And he couldn't pick up the phone if he was so worried
He had to call in at Sorrel Cottage two or three times
week? And it *was* two or three times a week, according t
Mardi. 'Have you ever thought...?' Connie paused an
cleared her throat. 'Have you ever considered you migh
feel better if you had a man in your life?'

'Good grief, no!' Bethany laughed. 'I had one for seven years. I don't want another one.'

Damn. That didn't sound at all promising, but Connie wasn't the kind of woman to give up easily. 'Not even one to cuddle up to when times get rough?'

'I've got Tiny for that,' Bethany replied, her grey eyes dancing, 'and unlike your average man he doesn't sulk or complain.'

'You're as bad as my brother,' Connie complained. 'He won't date anyone either.'

'Maybe he's happy on his own, like me.'

'Rubbish! He's still carrying a torch for Sarah Taunton, and heaven alone knows why. He only went out with the girl a few times...'

Sometimes all it took was one look, Bethany thought, remembering the night she'd met Jake. She'd been at a very dull party with friends and had just decided to make her excuses when he'd arrived. Their eyes had met, she'd found herself walking across the room towards him, and...

'And I don't think I'm being unreasonable, do you, Bethany?'

'I...um...I—I'm sure you're not,' she stammered, wondering what on earth Connie had been talking about.

'Simon says I should mind my own business. Michael says the same only not so politely, but he's my brother, Bethany. I want to see him married and settled.'

'I expect he'll meet some nice young girl soon,' she replied encouragingly.

The prospect didn't appear to afford Connie much pleasure. 'Michael doesn't need a nice young girl. He needs a woman—a proper, grown-up, mature woman. A woman like—' Hot colour stained her cheeks as her eyes met Bethany's. 'Simon was right,' she muttered, biting her lip. 'It's none of my business.'

'Connie—'

'Forget I said anything—forget I even mentioned it.'

'But—'

'I want to ask you about something else anyway—something that is very much my business. I want to know... I'd like to find out...' Connie's cheeks darkened to crimson and she laughed a little shakily. 'Oh, hell, why on earth am I pussy-footing around like this? Simon and I have been married for eight years, and we're not childless from choice. What I want to know is...would herbalism or aromatherapy help me?'

Bethany stared at her with ill-concealed dismay. 'Have you talked to Simon about this, Connie?'

She shook her head. 'And I haven't discussed it with Michael either. Bethany, I know you can't perform miracles, but if there's even the remotest chance you can help me I want you to try.'

'But—'

'If Michael weren't my brother, would you be hesitating for a second?'

A rueful smile curved Bethany lips. 'You know I wouldn't, but you also know how he feels about herbalism.'

'He's letting you treat Linda Balfour,' Connie protested. 'Bethany, please, I want you to take me on as a patient.'

Her large blue eyes were anxious, pleading, and Bethany groaned inwardly. Michael might have mellowed slightly towards her profession lately but he'd blow a fuse if he found out she was treating his sister—and he *would* find out. Orkney was too small a place for secrets.

'Connie, I don't want— The very last thing I want is to raise your hopes.'

Connie stared at her silently for a moment, then smiled. A small, crooked, slightly bitter smile. 'Bethany, I've had blood scans, X-rays, ultrasound scans and laparoscopies. I've been poked and prodded about by total strangers who have spent more time between my legs than my husband has, and it's all been for nothing. I don't have any hopes left, only impossible dreams.'

It was that smile which persuaded Bethany. The smile which clearly hid years of heartache and longing, and before she could allow herself to think about what Michael would say, she said quickly, 'When would you want to start?'

'How about now—if you can fit me in?' Connie replied, eagerness plain in her voice.

Bethany glanced at her watch. 'My next patient isn't due until eleven…'

'Then what are we waiting for?' Connie declared.

You said the consultant in Glasgow diagnosed unexplained infertility?' Bethany asked after she'd given Connie a thorough examination.

Connie nodded. 'Apparently, you can have all the right plumbing, it's pumping out everything it should, but for some unknown reason you just don't get pregnant.'

'How's your menstrual cycle?'

'Regular as clockwork. And before you ask, Simon and I have tried having intercourse on the thirteenth, fourteenth, and fifteenth day before my period, taking my temperature daily to check I was ovulating, putting pillows under my hips when we were making love—'

'You've really been through the mill, haven't you?' Bethany broke in sympathetically.

Connie sighed. 'You could say that.'

'Then the first thing I want you to do is massage rose, geranium and nutmeg oil into your skin every day. Top to toe is best, in a carrier oil like sweet almond. Not only will it help you to relax but rose in particular has a special affinity with the female sex organs.' Bethany reached into her drawer and took out a prescription pad. 'I'll write down how much I want you to use, but don't, for heaven's sake, be tempted to exceed it. Too much isn't good for you.'

'Massage myself every day.' Connie nodded. 'OK, what next?'

'Wild yam is traditionally linked with the regulation o female hormones, and false unicorn stimulates the ovarie themselves.' Bethany frowned. 'But I think I'll start yo off on agnus castus first. The ancient Greeks used to us the leaves from the tree to encourage the pituitary gland t stimulate the hormones involved in ovulation.'

'Sounds quite exotic.' Connie laughed a little nervously

'Not really.' Bethany smiled. 'A rosemary compoun would also help to maintain your hormone balance. I'l make you up some tinctures—that just involves me soakin the leaves in alcohol—but I'd better warn you they tast pretty foul.'

'What medicine doesn't?' Connie chuckled.

Michael's sister looked so eager, so hopeful, tha Bethany hated to bring her down to earth, but knew sh must. 'Connie, you do understand you could take all th things I prescribe and nothing might happen?'

'Of course I understand,' she replied brightly, bu Bethany wasn't one bit deceived. She'd treated patient with unexplained infertility in Winchester, and they'd al said they'd understood that herbs couldn't achieve miracle and had then been completely devastated when they hadn' become pregnant.

All she could hope was that for Michael's sister the treat ment would work. And she could hope even more fervently as she waved Connie goodbye and ushered Anne Bichai through to her consulting room for her weekly Saturda massage, that Michael wouldn't discover what she was do ing for a very long time. Asking her to see what she coul do for Linda Balfour's CFS was one thing. Treating hi sister was something else.

'How are you getting on with the self-help massage tech niques I showed you, Anne?' Bethany asked as the gir slipped off her blouse.

'Not very well, I'm afraid. I seem to be all fingers an thumbs.'

'Persevere with it,' Bethany said encouragingly. 'Lifting patients, bending, being on your feet all day in A and E—it's really put a strain on your back, and if you're not careful you could end up with a lot of problems when you're older.'

'Try telling that to Mr Wilkie, the consultant in charge of A and E,' Anne said ruefully as she got onto the massage table. 'He caught me doing one of the exercises you recommended the other day and I thought he was going to expire on the spot.'

'Was it the one where you have to throw your chest out as far as you can?' Bethany laughed. 'I bet—'

'Sorry to disturb you, Mrs Seton,' Mardi interrupted, popping her head round the consulting-room door, 'but Dr Harcus is here and wants to know if you could spare him some time.'

Her receptionist's face spoke volumes and Bethany gave her a very hard stare. It was one thing for Mardi to tease her in private about Michael's many visits—and even that wasn't funny any more—but now she had Anne Bichan looking at her with keen interest, too.

'Tell him…' She bit her lip. 'Tell him I'm sorry but I'm really booked solid today.'

'He thought you might be,' Mardi said blithely, 'so he said to tell you he doesn't mind waiting. He's off duty this weekend, you see.'

Which left her right back where she'd started.

Why, oh, why did life have to be so darned complicated? Bethany wondered as she nodded with as much casual indifference as she could muster, only to see Mardi and Anne exchange glances. She really enjoyed Michael's visits and yet now she was going to have to find some tactful way of telling him not to come so often, and all because nobody could believe that she and Michael could possibly be just friends.

\*    \*    \*

'Alistair, if you could empty the wheelbarrow for me, I'l start on this patch now,' Michael declared as he peeled of his sweat-soaked shirt and reached for the spade again.

'Couldn't we just sit in the sun and talk about th Norsemen and their longships instead?' Alistair grumbled

'Work first—talk later,' Michael replied, then grinned a the boy sighed deeply. 'Look on the bright side, sport. W might find some buried Norse artefacts if we dig dee enough.'

Alistair's face brightened immediately. 'Hey, I neve thought of that. Do you think we might? I mean—'

'I'm bored with weeding,' Katie announced, throwing away the daisy chain she'd been making. 'Why can't I push the wheelbarrow, or do some of the digging instead?'

'Because girls don't dig,' her brother replied scornfully 'It's men's work.'

'Is not!' she threw back at him as he began pushing th wheelbarrow to the far corner of the garden. 'Mummy's girl, and she's always digging in the garden.'

Don't I know it, Michael thought ruefully. He'd tol Bethany time and time again that what she really neede for her garden was a bulldozer, but did she listen? Did she heck!

'Why are you digging up Mummy's garden anyway Michael?' Katie continued, turning to him. 'You're a doc tor, not a gardener.'

Too right he was, but the thought of Bethany out her half killing herself... 'I'm a friend of your mummy's, an friends like to help.'

Katie digested this for a moment, then frowned. 'Ralph Elliot's a friend of Mummy's, but he doesn't work in th garden.'

'Ralph Elliot?' Michael repeated, his brows lowering.

'He gives me sweets when he comes for his massage Alistair doesn't like him, but I think he's funny. I hear Mummy telling Mardi he was a groper. What's a groper?

'Somebody…somebody who has poor eyesight, and worse judgement,' Michael muttered, heeling his spade into the ground grimly. Why the hell hadn't Bethany told him Ralph was bothering her? He could have sorted him out. In fact, he'd like nothing better than to sort him out. Katie—'

'Mummy said she's going to take us out tomorrow if the weather's good, and we get the car back from the garage.'

'Your car's broken down again?' Michael exclaimed, momentarily distracted.

'It's always breaking down,' she said with a sigh. 'Eric says it's an old crock.'

'Katie, about Ralph Elliot…'

'I've got to go.' She was already off and running. 'It's lunchtime and Mummy looks cross.'

Hot and cross, and absolutely wonderful, Michael decided as he turned and saw her, and felt the familiar lurch of his heart.

How could he ever have thought she wasn't beautiful? he wondered as he watched her ushering the children into the house. OK, so she didn't possess the conventional good looks beloved of the film industry, and she wasn't pencil-slim like the models in the glossy magazines, but his dreams weren't plagued by images of picture-perfect film stars and anorexic models.

His dreams were disturbed by a lush, hourglass figure, a wealth of auburn hair and a pair of large grey eyes that sparkled and danced even when they were shooting daggers at him, which they were doing now as she stormed up to him.

'Michael, what the hell do you think you're doing?'

'And hello, and good morning to you, too, Bethany.' He grinned, turning over another clump of earth.

'Will you put down that spade at once?' she demanded angrily. 'Don't you realise how much damage you could be doing to your shoulder?'

'My shoulder's fine.'

And he had X-ray vision, did he? If he'd let her trea
it—but no. He'd elected to go to a masseur on the mainlan
instead—to somebody she'd never heard of who could hav
done irreparable damage to his shoulder muscles for all h
knew.

Oh, come on, Bethany, her mind protested as she trie
her best to glare at him, only to find herself mesmerised b
the tiny beads of sweat shimmering and glistening on hi
muscular chest. It's not his lack of faith in your abilit
that's got you so rattled. It's seeing him like this in you
garden, looking so damn virile, so masculine, so…so in
tensely male.

'I didn't ask you to dig up my garden,' she said, draggin
her gaze away from his naked chest with difficulty. 'I don'
*want* you to dig my garden. What you're doing—it's no
right, it's not fitting. You're a doctor—'

'And how I spend my weekend off is my affair,' he sai
gently.

'Yes, but—'

'Bethany, we're friends. Are you saying there are limi
tations on that friendship?'

'Of course I'm not saying that,' she responded, strivin
for calm. But neither was she going to admit that the sigh
of him was doing the strangest things to her heart rate. 'An
you mustn't think I'm not grateful for your help, becaus
I am—'

'Then there's no problem, is there?' he said smilingly.

There shouldn't have been. She knew only too well tha
there shouldn't have been. Good grief, she massaged half
naked men every day and yet never before had her breath
felt as though it had been sucked right out of her lungs.

Well, of course it does, you ninny, she told herself an
grily. Michael Harcus is one very good-looking man, an
a woman would have to be blind not to be affected by th

sight of him stripped off in her garden. She would. She *would*.

'Mardi…Mardi said you wanted to talk to me about something,' she said, looking everywhere but at him. 'I'm sorry, but I'm really busy—'

'Aren't you going to have lunch?'

'I've only time for a sandwich and coffee.'

'Sounds great,' he replied, putting down his spade and reaching for his shirt.

She didn't recall offering him anything, but if it meant him covering up that unsettling wall of masculine flesh she was more than happy to oblige. 'Salad and tuna on rye suit you?'

'Sounds terrific.'

She doubted whether it would be terrific, but it would certainly be quick. And it needed to be. Saturdays were always busy, but today was turning out to be murder.

'You're not still worried about Linda Balfour, are you?' she asked when she'd made their sandwiches and switched on the kettle. 'I can assure you—'

'I came to thank you for sending William Oliver to me,' he interrupted, sitting down at the kitchen table. 'I've just found out that he has temporal arteritis.'

'That sounds serious,' she said, pausing as she reached for two mugs.

'It can be. It's quite a rare condition in which the walls of the arteries that pass over the temples in the scalp become inflamed, and if it's not diagnosed in time the patient can go blind.'

'And have you got it in time?' she asked with concern.

He nodded. 'I'm hoping so. I've started him on a course of corticosteroid. Most people with the disease respond to it very quickly and after a two-year course they're completely cured, so I'm keeping my fingers crossed. What I'm more interested in, however, is why you were so worried about him.'

She frowned as she spooned some coffee into the mugs. 'I honestly don't know. I knew his headache could have been caused by simple tension, and even when he told me he'd been feeling very tired lately with no appetite I was thinking, Hey, the man's sixty-five, Bethany, but...' She shook her head. 'I guess it was just a gut feeling.'

'Snap.' He smiled. 'When the CAT scan showed no abnormality—probably because the temporal arteritis isn't very advanced yet—I still wasn't happy so I asked him to come into the surgery so I could take some blood to do a CBC and ESR. The CBC results...' He came to a halt. She had started to laugh and his lips curved a little uncertainly. 'What? What's so funny?'

'Michael, I need a translation. I know a CAT scan takes X-rays of the brain, but a CBC, an ESR?'

'Sorry,' he said grinning. 'A CBC is a complete blood count and it measures the number of red and white cells and also the number of platelets in your blood. Usually if there's a serious problem the number of cells and platelets are low, but William's were completely normal.'

'But you still weren't happy?' she said.

'Like you, I couldn't rid myself of the feeling that I was missing something, and it was when I checked the ESR— the erythrocyte sedimentation rate—that I found it.'

'And how do you do an ESR?' she asked, taking a bite out of her sandwich, fascinated.

'It's not a difficult procedure. You simply mix a sample of the patient's blood with an anticoagulant to stop the blood from clotting, put your sample into a test tube and leave it for an hour. The red blood cells sink to the bottom of the tube, leaving the clear plasma at the top. A normal sediment rate would have been 20. William's was 100.'

'So that, coupled with the headache he's been suffering, told you he had temporal arteritis?'

He nodded.

'Ain't science wonderful? No, I mean it, Michael,' she

aid as he shook his head reprovingly at her. 'Being able
o diagnose something as serious as that from just a little
ample of blood—it's incredible.'

'So you admit orthodox medicine has its good points?'
e teased, but just as she began to chuckle he remembered
omething else. Something that wiped all amusement from
is face. 'Bethany, why didn't you tell me Ralph Elliot was
naking a nuisance of himself?'

'Making a nuisance...?' Her eyebrows snapped down.
'Mardi— Mardi's been talking to you, hasn't she?'

'No, but I wish she had. Bethany, the man's a drunk and
. womaniser, and I'll make sure he doesn't bother you
gain.'

'You'll do no such thing!' she cried, considerably
.larmed by the decidedly martial glint in his eye. 'Michael,
 can't afford to turn away patients—not even odious creeps
ike Ralph Elliot.'

'And neither should you be subjected to sexual harass-
nent at work!' he flared. God, just the thought of Ralph
Elliot touching her was enough to make him want to drive
traight over to the accountant's office and punch him
enseless. 'Does this happen often—men thinking you're
air game because you're a masseuse?'

'Of course it doesn't,' she protested. 'I get the occasional
oker—every masseuse does—but the vast majority of men
vould never dream of abusing the situation. Good grief, I
;ave you a massage, and I bet you didn't think of jumping
n me, did you?'

Oh, but he had, he remembered, feeling his cheeks
larken. Even now he couldn't forget the touch of her hands
n his body, and when she'd asked him to turn over...
Lord, did she know there was another, strictly non-medical
neaning to the word 'frottage'? He did, and just thinking
.bout it was enough to bring him out in a cold sweat.

'Bethany—'

'You asked me earlier if there were any limitations on

our friendship,' she interrupted. 'Well, I've just discovered one. Don't try to run my life.'

'I'm not—'

'You are!' she exclaimed, torn between amusement and anger. 'Good grief, between you wanting to organise my business and your sister trying to organise my social life, I'm lucky to have a life to call my own!'

Michael put down his sandwich uncomfortably. He had a pretty fair idea of what his sister might have been up to, and if he discovered she'd even mentioned his name he was going to strangle her. 'What's Connie been doing now?' he asked, with a casualness he was very far from feeling.

'She thinks I should start dating again,' she replied, rolling her eyes heavenwards to show just what she thought of that as an idea. 'She's convinced that all my troubles would be over if I just had a man in my life.'

He studied the plate in front of him with rapt interest. 'And you don't agree?'

'Of course I don't.' She laughed. 'Believe me, the last thing I want—or need—is a man in my life.'

Well, that was certainly clear enough, and he knew he should have left it there, but something impelled him to comment, 'That's a bit definite, isn't it?'

'I can be definite, Michael. I've got my children, my work and a new home. I can change a plug, mend a fuse, put up bookshelves—'

'Men have other uses apart from DIY, Bethany.'

He meant sex, she supposed, but frankly she thought it vastly overrated. Romantic novels might go on about exploding bubbles, soaring crescendos and mind-blowing orgasms but the reality, she'd found, tended to be a rather nice build-up followed by an almighty feeling of dissatisfaction.

'A man can't offer me anything I wouldn't just as happily live without,' she replied dismissively. 'And you've forgotten one thing,' she continued as Michael opened his mouth, clearly intending to argue. 'Even if I wanted to get involved with someone again—which I don't—how many men do you know who'd be willing to take on two children as part of the package?'

'I would,' he replied without thinking, then cursed himself the moment the words were out of his mouth. What the hell had made him say that? OK, so he was attracted to Bethany—more than attracted if the truth be told—but she wasn't looking for a brief affair, and he most certainly didn't want anything else. 'Bethany, what I just said—'

'Was downright stupid,' she snorted. 'Michael, I'd give you two months tops with Katie and Alistair and then you'd be begging for somebody—anybody—to take them away. Children aren't something you get on loan, to be sent back if you decide parenthood isn't for you. Children are for life.'

'My father was still telling me to wrap up well on cold days when I was twenty-two,' he said ruefully, and she smiled.

'Sounds like he was a good dad, your father.'

'He was,' he murmured, remembering.

'Well, you can take it from me there are precious few like him around,' she declared, trying and failing to keep the bitterness from her voice. 'Katie was thirteen months old when Jake left, and Alistair was not quite five.'

Furious anger darkened his face. 'What kind of scumbag leaves his wife for another woman when his children are only—'

'He didn't.'

'Sorry?'

'Jake didn't leave me for another woman, Michael,' she said gently as he gazed at her in confusion. 'He left because he got bored with playing Daddy, bored with coming home to two crying children and bored with living with a crabby, worn-out wife.' She took a sip of her coffee, not wanting to resurrect painful memories, but suddenly it seemed important that Michael should understand.

'Jake…he thought the children could be slotted into our lives, that we could go on living as we'd done before. When he realised there was more to being a dad than a nice photograph on his desk, he went out one night and didn't come back.'

'Oh, Bethany—'

'Don't.' She moistened her lips and gave him a too-bright smile. 'Please, don't pity me. Marriages end all the time, and mine wasn't the first and it certainly won't be the last.'

His mouth tightened, and he reached out and covered her hand with his. 'Nevertheless, I'm sorry—so very sorry.'

To her dismay tears welled in her eyes and she bit them back quickly. She hadn't cried since the divorce, hadn't allowed herself to, and yet now…

Now, as she stared down at Michael's hand, felt the warmth and strength of his fingers on hers, she knew that what she wanted most in the world was for him to hold her, to comfort her, and to tell her he'd make everything all right.

And it was crazy. She didn't need anything put right. She was happy— OK, maybe not exactly happy, but content. She had her work, her children…

'Bethany, you do know you're not alone now, don't you? That if you're in trouble I'll always be there for you?'

She looked up to find Michael's brown eyes on her, so gentle, so concerned, and in that split second felt something slip from her shoulders. The burden she'd carried since Jake had left. The burden of five years of worrying alone, of coping alone. She wouldn't have to do it on her own any more. Michael would be there. He'd said so, and she believed him.

'Thank you,' she murmured, her voice husky with unshed tears.

And Michael knew exactly what had happened, realised exactly what he'd promised, and didn't know whether to whoop with delight because she so clearly trusted him or to head for the door and never come back.

Commitment. The word echoed round and round in his head like a steel trap closing, but surely this wasn't commitment? Surely offering to help a friend in trouble was just human kindness?

Yeah, right, if you actually saw her as a friend, his mind pointed out, but you don't, do you? You might want to hug a friend, to comfort them, but you wouldn't want to hold on and never let go.

'Bethany—'

'Oops! Pardon me for interrupting!'

Bethany glanced over her shoulder to see her receptionist standing in the doorway, and shook her head in exasperation. 'Oh, for heaven's sake, Mardi, you're not interrupting anything. What's the problem?'

'Eric's phoned about your car, and I'm afraid—'

'He can't get it back to us until Tuesday,' Alistair interrupted, despair plain on his face as he pushed past the receptionist. 'We *have* to get it back today, Mum. You said you'd take us to Maeshowe and Skara Brae tomorrow. You *promised*.'

'Alistair, if the car can't be mended until Tuesday we'll just have to go next weekend.'

'But it might rain next weekend—you might be too busy next weekend!'

'Alistair, be sensible,' Bethany protested. 'What other alternative do we have?'

For a second her son said nothing, then his face lit up. 'Michael can take us. He told me last week it's ages since he's been to Maeshowe.'

'Alistair, I'm sure Michael has more important things to do than trail round the countryside with us on his day off,'

Bethany said firmly as Mardi made a strategic retreat with a 'who'd ever be a mother' look on her face.

'I bet he hasn't,' Alistair insisted. 'I bet he'd love to take us. You would, wouldn't you, Michael?' he added, turning to him.

Michael looked as though it was the very last thing he wanted to do, and who could blame him? Bethany thought ruefully. Ferrying her and the kids around Orkney's historic sites was hardly likely to be his idea of fun. 'Alistair, we'll go next weekend—'

'But if Michael takes us—'

'Michael is taking us nowhere,' she said determinedly. 'And I don't want to hear another word about it,' she added as her son opened his mouth to protest. 'Understand?'

'Oh, I understand all right!' he exclaimed, his eyes flashing. 'All you ever think about is work, and saving money and I think... I think you're *mean*!'

And before Bethany could stop him he slammed out of the kitchen, leaving her staring in mortified embarrassment at Michael.

'I...I don't know what to say,' she began. 'I'm really sorry about that.'

'Don't be,' Michael said dismissively. 'He was disappointed—it's understandable.'

'Yes, but trying to force you into doing something isn't. I'll bring him back, make him apologise.' She made for the door only to groan. 'Is that the time? I've a patient in five minutes—'

'Bethany, I don't want—or need—Alistair to apologise to me,' Michael declared.

She put a harassed hand to her forehead. 'But making a scene like that... I feel dreadful.'

'Then don't.' Lord, but she didn't need this, he thought as he gazed at her. She looked pale and tired enough already, without having more worries heaped on her shoulders. What she needed was a day out, a chance to relax. 'Bethany, about this trip to Maeshowe…'

'Forget about it. We'll go next weekend.'

'It might rain, as Alistair said.'

'Then we'll go the following weekend.' She managed a smile. 'It's not your problem, Michael.'

It wasn't, he knew it wasn't, and yet… 'I'll pick you up tomorrow at eleven.'

She stared at him in amazement. 'Michael, you can't possibly want to trail round Maeshowe and Skara Brae on your day off.'

He didn't. 'Of course I do—it'll be fun.'

'But, Michael—'

'Your next patient's waiting, Bethany.' And just to emphasise the point he strode over to the kitchen door and opened it. 'Tomorrow at eleven, OK?'

And no matter what she said, he wouldn't take no for an answer.

How could his sister say he was selfish? Bethany wondered as the rest of the day flew by in a blur of appointments. And as for Mardi… Hellfire and damnation, the way her receptionist carried on you'd have thought no woman was safe in his company, and yet Michael had never shown her anything but kindness, never done anything or said anything that had made her feel even remotely uncomfortable in his presence.

Well, OK, all right, when he'd been doing up her buttons at Connie's barbecue she might have felt a little bit uncomfortable. And perhaps the sight of him in her garden had been a bit unnerving, but that had only been because she'd overreacted, not because he'd been trying to seduce her.

Actually, no man in his right mind would want to seduce her, she thought with a sigh when the children were in bed and she'd run her bath. Not unless he was wearing a paper bag over his head so he couldn't see the roll of fat round her midriff and tummy.

Oh, what difference did it make what her body looked like? she told herself with irritation as she got into the bath. No man was ever going to see it again unless he was a doctor. Lord, no, she thought with horror as a face suddenly came into her mind—a face dominated by a pair of warm brown eyes and a deeply cleft chin. Not that doctor. Not even for a medical examination.

And why not? a little voice whispered.

Because he's a friend, that's why, she retorted, reaching for the soap, and you don't want your friends seeing your body, warts and all.

And is that the only reason? the voice persisted. It couldn't be perhaps that you've stopped seeing him simply as a friend and started seeing him as a man, could it?

'Rubbish!' she exclaimed to Katie's set of rubber ducks, which seemed to be suddenly smirking knowingly at her from the side of the bath. 'Rubbish, rubbish, *rubbish*!'

# CHAPTER FIVE

MICHAEL groaned inwardly as the door of Sorrel Cottage opened in answer to his knock and Bethany appeared dressed in a pair of hip-hugging blue jeans and a red T-shirt.

He should be certified.

Anyone who volunteered to spend a whole day in close proximity to the kind of body which ought to have a government health warning stamped on it should most definitely be certified.

'Ready to go?' he asked, schooling his expression into one of jovial *bonhomie* with difficulty.

'Sort of.' Bethany grimaced. 'Katie, Alistair—will you hurry up? Michael's here!'

Actually, he didn't need the government health warning, Michael decided as the children tumbled out of the house. Those two bundles of mischief would put a damper on even the most rampant libido. And if they didn't, Tiny sure as heck would, he thought with dismay as the dog bounded round the side of the house and made straight for the car.

'Alistair, Tiny is *not* coming with us,' Bethany protested.

'But he'll be lonely if we leave him at home,' her son protested. 'He loves going to the beach, swimming in the sea, and Michael doesn't mind, do you, Michael?'

Michael thought of his car's expensive upholstery and gritted his teeth. 'The more the merrier.'

'Are you sure?' Bethany said, gazing up at him uncertainly. 'Tiny's pretty big, and if he gets wet...'

'What's a little sea water and sand between friends?' Michael declared, trying hard not to wince as Tiny leapt into the front of his Mercedes, then scrabbled his way over into the back seat. 'Are these for the boot?' he added, pointing to the collection of plastic carrier bags sitting outside the cottage.

She nodded. 'It's just a few things we might need if the weather changes.'

He glanced up at the cloudless blue sky and his lips quirked. 'A natural-born optimist, I see.'

'Force of habit, more like,' she said with a chuckle. 'If I don't take everything bar the kitchen sink, we're bound to need it.'

From the weight of the bags he heaved into the boot Michael rather suspected the kitchen sink was already in one of them. 'Anything else?'

She shook her head. 'Not unless you've changed your mind about taking us.'

He wanted to change his mind. He wanted to tell her an emergency had come up, that Simon needed his help, but he couldn't. Not with a pair of large, direct grey eyes fixed on him.

'Of course I haven't,' he said brightly. 'In fact, I've been looking forward to this all morning.'

And she smiled—a wide, wonderful smile that did irreparable damage to his heart rate—and whispered, 'Liar. But thank you.'

'Bethany—'

'Mum, if we don't go soon we're not going to have enough time to see everything,' Alistair interrupted. 'My book on Skara Brae says you should spend at least two hours there if you really want to explore it thoroughly.'

Michael's eyes met Bethany's with such ill-disguised horror that she had to suck in her cheeks quickly to quell the laughter that threatened to overwhelm her. 'Two hours?' she repeated with scarcely a tremor. 'In that case, we'd better get going.'

'He's kidding—right?' Michael muttered as Alistair and Katie clambered into the car.

'I wish he was,' Bethany replied with feeling. 'Prepare to be bored out of your mind for the rest of the day, Dr Marcus!'

But he wasn't.

He wasn't bored when Katie entertained them all the way to Skara Brae with a selection of her favourite songs. He wasn't bored when Alistair dragged him round every one of the six prehistoric houses, demanding to know how the stone beds were made, what things would be stored in the stone dressers and if the doors were so low because the people were much shorter five thousand years ago than they were now.

He might have been exhausted, and bemused, but he certainly wasn't bored.

'I take my hat off to mothers everywhere,' he said ruefully when Alistair finally let him off the hook and went in search of the guide to bombard him with questions about the finer points of the village's construction. 'You all deserve medals.'

'I was just going to say the same thing about you.' Bethany chuckled as she followed him out of the village and down onto the beach below. 'For a confirmed bachelor you're pretty good with children.'

He turned in surprise. 'Who told you I was a confirmed bachelor?'

'Well, you are, aren't you?' she countered, her eyes dancing.

He'd always thought he was. He was always telling his sister he was, but... 'You haven't answered my question,' he said, playing for time.

She laughed—a deep rich chuckle that had him clenching his jaw against the effect it had on him. 'Michael, I don't need anyone to tell me. When a man's had as many girlfriends as you've had, it's obvious.'

He managed to laugh, but only just. Never would he have thought he could have found himself wishing he didn't have a past, but he wished it now. 'Bethany, the stories you may have heard about me…ninety per cent of them are exaggerated.'

'Ninety per cent?' she queried, her eyebrows rising quizzically.

'OK, make that seventy per cent,' he conceded awkwardly, 'but we've all done foolish things in our youth.'

'Oh, you poor old man,' she mocked, but when a flush of dark colour appeared on his cheeks she put her hand on his arm reassuringly. 'Michael, I don't give a button about your reputation. We're friends, remember, and friends don' judge one another.'

'Yes, but—'

'And it's not as though I've any cause for concern. know I'm not your type.'

He wanted to ask if he could ever be hers, but he didn' dare.

Once he would have. Once he would have said something slick, glib, guaranteed to make any woman blush and melt into his arms, but he couldn't—wouldn't—play those sorts of games with Bethany. And playing games with women, he realised ruefully as he stared down at her hand a hand that looked so small and vulnerable on his arm, was all he knew how to do.

'Bethany—'

'Oh, wouldn't you just know it?' she groaned, hearing the sound of raised voices behind her. 'Alistair and Katie are fighting again.'

'Connie and I used to fight all the time when we were kids,' he replied as Katie flew past them, her small cheeks red with fury, with Alistair and Tiny in hot pursuit. 'Still do, come to think of it.'

'Then you don't think…' She paused and bit her lip 'You don't think it's because I can't spend enough time with them, being a single parent, having to work—'

'Bethany, *all* kids fight,' he interrupted. 'And your children seem perfectly well adjusted to me.'

She smiled a little crookedly. 'I hope they are. I pray they are. But I can't help worrying about them—not having a dad around…'

'That's scarcely your fault,' he said grimly. 'You weren't the one who walked out—Jake was.'

'Yes, but maybe if I'd tried a little harder, been more tolerant, maybe he wouldn't have left.'

A thought came into his mind—a thought he discovered he didn't like one bit but knew he had to voice. 'Do you…? Are you still in love with him?'

Was she? For the last five years she'd been too busy simply trying to survive even to think about it. She could remember her devastation when Jake had left, then how angry she'd been, but now… Now, when she tried to picture him, all she saw was a blurry outline.

'I don't think so,' she murmured, her eyes fixed on Alistair and Katie who were throwing sticks for Tiny, their argument apparently forgotten. 'He's the children's father—he'll always be that—but, no, I don't love him any more. I did once. Oh, yes, I did…once.'

Michael gazed at her impotently. He hated it when her eyes clouded with remembered unhappiness. Hated to think she'd ever been unhappy at all. A woman like her should never have been unhappy. She should have always been cherished and adored and loved.

'It's almost one o'clock,' he said quickly, trying to bring her back to him, back to the present. 'What are we doing about lunch?'

For a second he didn't think she'd heard him, then she blinked and smiled. 'I thought we might have lunch on the beach. I made a few sandwiches—'

'Forget the sandwiches. I've brought something a whole lot more exciting.'

And he had.

'Oh, Michael, you really shouldn't have,' she gasped when he produced a tantalising array of cold meats, poached salmon, crusty rolls and salad from a hamper in the boot of his car. 'But—'

'Can I tempt you?' His eyebrows rose quizzically.

'You bet,' she breathed. 'It looks wonderful.'

And it was. Even Katie, usually so picky about her food, ate everything she was given, and Alistair, who generally had to be bullied into keeping his carbohydrate level high because of his diabetes, ate three of the strawberry tarts Michael had brought as a pudding.

'You're a man of many talents, Michael,' Bethany observed when the children took Tiny down to the water's edge to cool off, and she relaxed contentedly on the blanket he had spread over the sand. 'Doctor, chef—'

'Not me,' he replied without thinking. 'The Lynnfield Hotel supplied all the food.'

'Then you must let me reimburse you,' she said immediately. 'I know how expensive hotels can be, and to have a whole meal—'

'Forget it, Bethany,' he interrupted, cursing himself inwardly for having lacked the foresight to lie and say he'd cooked all the food. 'It's my treat.'

'But it's too much,' she protested. 'I'm already in your debt, what with the petrol to get us here, the cost of admission to Skara Brae—'

'Perhaps you'd be happier if I gave you a fully itemised bill at the end of the day?' he snapped, and she flushed.

'I've upset you now, haven't I? I didn't mean to—but you've been so very good to us, and I'm so very grateful—'

'I don't want your damn gratitude!'

Startled by the harshness in his voice, she looked up at him, doubt and some dismay in her face, and for a second his own face was inscrutable, then he smiled. 'I find gratitude tedious, and if you persist in offering it I'll make you walk home.'

Her jaw dropped. 'Y-you wouldn't!'

'Don't bet on it,' he warned, but when a peal of laughter came from her something twisted inside him, something so acute it was almost a physical pain.

Lord, but he wanted this woman. Wanted to kiss her until she couldn't even remember her ex-husband's name, far less how badly he'd hurt her. Wanted to slide her T-shirt and jeans from her body and trace her soft curves with his lips and fingers. Wanted to lay her gently down on the rug and make love to her until the moon replaced the sun in the sky.

'Bethany—'

'Is there a rubbish bin on the beach, Michael, or do we have to take our litter home with us?'

For a second he gazed at her, open-mouthed, not knowing whether he wanted to laugh or strangle her. His body was aching—throbbing—with desire for her, and what was she thinking about? Garbage.

'There's a rubbish bin at the car park,' he said abruptly.

'Michael—'

'The children seem to be wandering a bit far away from us,' he continued, getting to his feet. 'I'll bring them back.'

'But—'

He was already striding away, and she gazed after him in confusion. He looked…not exactly angry, more confused and not a little hurt.

His face had borne the same expression earlier, she remembered, when she'd commented on his reputation. Lord, he didn't really think she cared about it, did he? She didn't give a damn about his reputation, or about how many girlfriends he'd had or would have in the future.

Oh, really? her mind whispered as her eyes caressed the broad sweep of his back, the long line of his muscular, tanned legs.

Yes, really, she argued back. His private life is absolutely none of my business.

So if he started dating someone tomorrow it wouldn't bother you? her mind demanded.

Of course it wouldn't. He was a friend, and you didn't own your friends. So it wouldn't bother her. Not in the least. Not even a little bit. No. It wouldn't.

'Excuse me, dear, but would you happen to know how far it is to Row Head?'

Bethany jumped at the unexpected sound of a gentle voice, and turned to see an elderly woman gazing enquiringly at her. 'A-about three miles, I think,' she stammered, gathering her scattered wits together with difficulty. 'Maybe a little more.'

The woman sighed and mopped her forehead with her handkerchief. 'Too far for me, I'm afraid. My name's Wallace, by the way—Elsie Wallace.'

'Bethany Seton. Are you here on holiday?' she enquired, sensing the old lady's loneliness.

'More a sort of pilgrimage. I met my husband here when we were both stationed at Scapa Flow during the Second World War. We always planned to come back, but Ted— my husband—died last year.'

'Oh, I'm so sorry—'

'Don't be,' the woman interrupted. 'We had fifty happy years together and not many people are so blessed. Is that your son and daughter?' she continued as a shriek of laughter split the air, and Bethany turned to see Michael whirling Katie around in his arms with Alistair urging him on.

She nodded and the woman smiled. 'You have a lovely family, dear, you and your husband.'

And before Bethany could correct her, she'd walked away.

It had been a perfectly natural mistake to make, of course, Bethany told herself with a chuckle. A man, a woman, two children on a beach. People were bound to assume they were a family, but as she glanced back to where Michael had been playing with the children, her laughter died in her throat.

Michael wasn't whirling Katie around any more. She was standing beside him, her small arms wrapped round his knees, and he was listening intently to something Alistair was saying. And suddenly Bethany saw what the woman must have. How right he looked with them. How comfortable and at ease he looked with them. How like…how like a dad.

*No!* The word reverberated round and round in her head as she jumped to her feet and blindly began thrusting the remnants of their picnic into Michael's hamper. Michael wasn't the children's father. She didn't want him to be their father. They had one. They didn't need another one. Not now, not ever.

'Something wrong, Bethany?' Michael asked with concern as he came in answer to her wave, his gaze taking in her flushed cheeks, the way she wasn't quite meeting his eyes.

'Of course not,' she replied in an over-bright voice, 'but if Alistair wants to see Maeshowe…'

'Smart thinking, Mum,' her son nodded, unwittingly coming to her rescue. 'A bus party might arrive and I don't want to see it with hordes of people there. I want to see it when it's quiet.'

And I want to go home, Bethany thought wretchedly, and then was angry with herself for her reaction. Why was she getting so upset because Michael looked so comfortable with her children? She should be pleased they had a man in their lives, a man they could like and respect.

But that isn't what's upset you, is it? her mind whispered as Michael drove them to Maeshowe, with Alistair talking nineteen to the dozen about what they would see there. What's upset you—horrified you—is the realisation that if you let down your guard you could all too easily fall in love with this man.

And it was madness. After Jake had left she'd vowed she'd never let another man get close enough to hurt her and to find herself attracted to Michael... Lord, he'd split his sides laughing if he ever found out.

So he mustn't ever find out, and she...she had to pull herself together, and stop thinking such foolish thoughts.

And never ever let him take her and the children any where again, she decided with a groan when they arrived at Maeshowe and the middle-aged guide's eyes darted spec ulatively from her and the children to Michael so he had no option but to introduce them.

Well, it was too late now to wish she hadn't come. Too late to see the inevitable interpretation that Connie, and Mardi, and people like the guide, Mrs Mackay, would put on a simple day out, but that didn't mean she wouldn't learn by her mistake. Today was the first and last time she'd ever let Michael take her anywhere.

'Before we go inside,' Mrs Mackay declared as Bethany smiled across at Elsie Wallace who had clearly decided that perhaps a visit to Maeshowe might make up for the dis appointment of not seeing Row Head, 'I have to ask if anybody here suffers from claustrophobia or back trouble. There's no lighting inside the tomb, you see, and while the entrance passage is 14.5 metres long, it's only 1.4 metres high.'

No one said a word and with a brief nod Mrs Mackay picked up a lantern connected to a huge reel of cable and led the way into the tomb.

'Maeshowe is considered to be one of the finest prehis toric sites in Europe,' the guide continued once they'd all assembled around her in the inner chamber, having nego tiated the narrow passageway. 'It's at least five thousand years old, and when the tomb was opened in 1861 it was found to be empty apart from a single piece of human skull.'

'Oh, yuck!' Katie shuddered with distaste.

'Yuck, nothing,' her brother protested. 'Whose skull was it?'

'Nobody knows,' Mrs Mackay replied. 'All we do know is that some very important people must have been buried here, and according to the Vikings, who broke into the tomb in the twelfth century, a huge treasure was buried with them.' She pointed to the wall behind her and held up her light. 'Can you all see the lines cut into the stone? These are runes—a primitive type of Norse alphabet.'

'You mean this is writing?' Katie said, moving forward eagerly. 'Michael, lift me up—I can't see.'

Obediently he hoisted her up on his shoulder and the guide ran her finger along one section of the runes. 'This one says, "Haakon single-handed bore treasures from this howe", and this one here says, "These runes were carved by the man most skilled in runes on the Western Ocean, with the axe that killed Gaukr Trandkill's son in the South of Iceland."'

'And look at this, Katie,' Michael said, pointing to the wall beside him.

'It's a dragon,' she gasped with delight. 'And that's a walrus.'

'And here's a serpent,' Alistair enthused. 'But they're so small—I thought from my book they'd be huge.'

'When you consider they were probably carved with axes and knives, the detail is even more incredible,' Mrs Mackay commented, then frowned slightly. 'Are you feeling all right, Mrs Wallace?'

Elsie Wallace certainly didn't look 'all right'. Her face was white and drawn, and there were tiny beads of sweat on her lined forehead.

'I'm sorry, but I think I'll have to leave,' she murmured, pressing a handkerchief to her lips. 'I didn't think I was claustrophobic—Lord knows, I was in smaller, darker places than this during the War—but I need to leave now.'

Mrs Mackay gazed at her over her half-moon glasses

with some dismay and not a little vexation. 'This really is most awkward. We've only just arrived, and now we're all going to have to leave again.'

'Not necessarily,' Michael said smoothly. 'Do you have a spare lantern, Jean?'

'Only an emergency hurricane lamp—'

'Then I suggest you leave it with us and take the lady outside.'

It made sense, or at least it did until Katie and Alistair decided they wanted to go outside, too.

'It's fun going through the passage.' Katie beamed. 'Like being in an Indiana Jones movie.'

Mrs Mackay obviously disagreed with her and Bethany couldn't blame her. The fewer people in the passage the easier it would be for the guide to take Elsie Wallace outside again, but how Katie would react if she remained in the tomb with only a hurricane lamp for light was anybody's guess.

'OK, you can go,' Bethany said reluctantly, 'but the pair of you must come straight back in again with Mrs Mackay.'

'They'll be OK, Bethany,' Michael said, clearly sensing her unease when Katie and Alistair dashed off down the passage, with Mrs Mackay and Elsie Wallace following slowly behind them. 'Jean Mackay used to be a school-teacher before she took early retirement.'

'Sometimes I wish mothers could take early retirement,' she said with a sigh, and he laughed.

'Come and have a look at the rest of these runes,' he urged. 'They're actually quite fascinating. Look, this one says, "Many a woman has come stooping in here no matter how pompous a person she was."'

'He didn't like women very much, did he?' She couldn't help but laugh.

'And this one...' He held the hurricane lamp higher. 'This one says, "Ingigerd is the most beautiful of women."'

'And he clearly liked women too much,' she observed.
I bet that one was carved by a twelfth-century Casanova.'

'Or by a man deeply in love.'

His voice sounded deeper, husky, in the stillness, and a
small shiver ran down her back. She'd read in one of
Alistair's books on Orkney that it wasn't just the place
names that reflected the Norse influence, but the faces of
the people, too. She hadn't thought of it before but now,
seeing Michael's tanned face illuminated by the flickering
light of the hurricane lamp, she knew it was true.

He looked like a Viking warrior. He looked dangerous,
and unpredictable, and... And suddenly there didn't seem
to be enough air in the chamber.

This is silly, she told herself, gripping her hands tightly
together. He's a friend, only a friend. If Mrs Wallace hadn't
made that comment on the beach you would never have
thought of him as anything else, and yet now, alone with
him here, in the dark...

'Bethany, is there something wrong?'

A puzzled frown was creasing his forehead and she tried
to say she was fine but no words would come. She tried to
look away, to evade his eyes, so piercing and penetrating
even in the pale glow of the hurricane lamp, and found that
she couldn't.

'Bethany...?'

He hadn't moved. She knew he hadn't moved, and yet
he seemed much closer. Quickly she took a steadying
breath and wished she hadn't. She could smell the warmth
and sunshine of the day on his skin, the sharp, sweet scent
of pine soap and something altogether more subtly personal
and masculine. 'Michael...I think...I think...'

Slowly he reached out and touched her lower lip with
his finger, barely brushing the edge, but when he ran the
same finger along his own lip a shudder of sensation ran
down her spine, pooling and centring deep in her stomach.

'Bethany.' His voice was little more than a ragged whisper in the stillness. 'Bethany, I...'

She never did find out what he'd been going to say because before she could ask he had cupped her face between his broad, warm hands and his lips were on hers.

And it was like nothing she had ever experienced. It was like being struck by lightning, like drowning in warm oil as his tongue slipped inside her mouth, tasting, exploring, and his hands slid up her back, bringing her closer to him so her breasts were pressed against his chest and her nipples hardened instantly.

*Not safe—not safe!* The words shrieked in her head as she felt his body stirring against hers and felt her own trembling response. *Not safe—not safe!* it repeated as she heard a moan in the stillness and realised it had come from her own throat.

What was she doing—what was he doing? She didn't want this—she had never wanted this—and with an appalled gasp she jerked her mouth away from his, her heart beating frantically in her throat, her eyes wider and more appealing than she could ever have known. 'Michael, I...we...you shouldn't—'

'I didn't mean—'

'You don't have to apologise—'

'I apologise.'

Hell, but his voice sounded unsteady. *He* was unsteady, he realised as he bent to retrieve the hurricane lamp. His heart was pounding against his ribcage as though he'd just run a four-minute mile and he was acutely and uncomfortably aware of the unresolved ache deep in the pit of his stomach, but it was the look of horror on Bethany's face that really stunned him.

Kissing her had clearly been a big mistake. Kissing her had made her aware that he might actually see her as a woman, rather than as a friend, and it was obviously the last thing she wanted. Somehow he had to retrieve the situation

uation. Somehow he had to make her think what had just happened was unimportant, trivial, or he knew he would lose the little he had of her.

'I don't know why I just did that,' he declared, attempting a laugh that sounded false even to his own ears. 'I think there must be something in this place—the air, the atmosphere...' He bit his lip. 'Bethany, I'm sorry—truly sorry. That was a stupid thing to do.'

Then why did you do it? That was the obvious reply but she didn't say it. She didn't say anything, not even when Mrs Mackay's frightened voice echoed down the passage towards them.

'Dr Harcus, could you come quickly? The elderly lady who was in there with you—she's just collapsed!'

For a second neither of them moved, then with a muttered oath Michael turned on his heel and headed down the passage, leaving Bethany to follow him, her legs trembling, her brain in a whirl.

'I...I'm so sorry,' Elsie Wallace gasped when they reached her, her face wet with sweat and pain. 'Spoiling everyone's enjoyment like this—'

'Forget it.' Michael smiled as he pulled his medical bag out of the boot of his car, then got down on his knees beside her. 'Has anything like this ever happened to you before?'

'I had a small heart attack two years go,' Elsie replied, fear plain in her eyes as she clutched at her chest. 'Do you think this could be another one?'

'Michael...'

He heard the warning note in Bethany's voice and looked up to see her children watching him, their faces white with horrified fascination.

'Alistair, Katie, could you run to the end of the road for me?' he said immediately. 'I'm going to phone for an ambulance for Mrs Wallace and I'll need someone to direct them when they arrive.'

'I'm sure I don't need an ambulance,' Elsie protested as

the children dashed off without a backward glance. 'All I need—'

'Is to stop worrying and relax,' he urged.

And she needed to relax, he thought grimly as he took her blood pressure and pulse. A BP of 130 over 90 and a pulse rate of 100 wasn't good.

'I'm going to give you some morphine to ease your pain, Mrs Wallace,' he continued, taking a syringe out of his bag. 'And if you could just slip this pill under your tongue for me.'

The pill was nitroglycerine. With luck it would dilate the arteries around her heart, increasing the blood flow and oxygen to the heart, while the morphine should lessen her pain and therefore her anxiety. The only problem, as Michael knew only too well, was that both nitro and morphine dilated the blood vessels everywhere, not just around the heart, and it could lower Mrs Wallace's blood pressure too much. With less blood flowing to her brain and heart there was a very strong possibility she could have a bigger heart attack.

'She really needs a nitro drip and heparin to make her blood flow more easily,' Michael murmured to Bethany, sitting back on his heels, keeping his gaze fixed on the elderly woman. 'Hopefully the ambulance will arrive soon. I told them it's a priority one—'

'Oh, my God!' Mrs Mackay gasped as Elsie Wallace suddenly convulsed and lay still.

Without a word Michael leant over and whacked the elderly lady hard in the chest with his fist.

'*Dr Harcus!*' Mrs Mackay protested. 'Stop that at once! The poor woman—'

'Will you get out of my way?' he snapped, shrugging off her restraining hand impatiently.

'But—'

'I'm trying to create a small electrical current across her

hest to start her heart beating again!' he retorted as the
uide stared at him, appalled.

'Yes, but hitting her…'

'You'd rather she just died quietly?' he flared, and Mrs
Mackay promptly burst into tears.

'She's breathing again, Michael!' Bethany exclaimed
with relief, seeing Elsie's chest begin to rise and fall.

'But her breaths are too shallow.' He frowned, quickly
peeling off the sterile cover of the long polystyrene tube
he'd taken from his bag. 'I'll have to tube her.'

'Is there anything I can do?' Bethany asked. She was
damned if he was going to think her as useless as Mrs
Mackay who was quietly sobbing.

Swiftly he opened Elsie Wallace's mouth, slipped the
tube down into her trachea, then attached the end of the
tube to an ambu-bag. 'Could you keep squeezing the bag
for me while I check that the tube's in the right place?'

'How fast should I squeeze it?' she asked uncertainly.

'To the count of one…one…one.' He placed his stethoscope on Elsie's thin chest and listened. 'Her breath sounds
seem OK but we really need an X-ray to know for sure.'

'She's very white, Michael,' Bethany observed, squeezing the ambu-bag as though her life depended on it, though
she knew it wasn't her life but Elsie's.

'The time to worry is when she starts to go blue,' he
said tightly. 'Damn, her BP's down to 70 over 40. Where
s that damn ambulance?'

As though on cue, Bethany heard the sound of a wailing
siren in the distance and sent up a silent prayer of thanks.

'Do you want to go with Mrs Wallace, Michael?' one of
the paramedics asked, after the old lady had been gently
lifted into the ambulance.

'I've got to get Bethany and her children home first,'
Michael answered, clearly torn.

'There's no need,' she said quickly. 'If you loan me your
mobile I can phone for a taxi.'

'I can't let you do that—'

'Don't be silly—'

'But—'

'Mrs Wallace needs you more than we do right now. Don't worry, we'll be fine.''

'Bethany, this isn't right,' Michael exclaimed. 'Abandoning you and the kids...'

'It's OK,' she said firmly, wishing Michael would just get into his car and leave her to get her scrambled emotions under control.

'But—'

'The paramedics are waiting for you to follow them,' she said. 'Just lend me your phone.'

Realising that he'd lost the argument, he handed over his mobile. Before he could say any more, Bethany started to punch the number of a local taxi firm into it.

'Wow, but was that exciting or what?' Alistair breathed, his eyes shining.

'She will be all right, won't she—the old lady, I mean?' Katie asked, staring worriedly at the fast disappearing ambulance.

'Of course she will,' Bethany said, as she finished her call.

Ten minutes later the taxi arrived and they all piled in, with the children chattering excitedly about what had happened. Bethany stared blindly out at the passing countryside and tried to forget the way her mouth had opened willingly under Michael's lips. Tried to forget the way her heart had pounded and her knees had buckled. And tried hard—very hard—to forget the overwhelming surge of desire that had flooded through her as he'd held her close.

# CHAPTER SIX

MICHAEL pulled his stethoscope from his ears with a frown. 'Your bronchitis isn't getting any better, Mary.'

'It's this heat, Doctor,' she wheezed, her plump, florid face resigned, mournful. 'It really takes it out of you.'

It wasn't particularly warm. In fact, it was quite chilly for August, and Michael's frown deepened. 'Have you been using the bronchodilator I gave you?'

'Don't ever leave home without it, Doctor.'

He doubted it. Mary Cassidy was the most disorganised person he'd ever met, and for a split second he was tempted to call her bluff and ask her to produce the inhaler, only to decide it wasn't worth it. 'The diet sheet I gave you—are you following it religiously?'

'To the letter.' She nodded.

'Then let's see how much you weigh today,' he said, walking across to the consulting-room scales, leaving Mary with no choice but to follow him. That she was reluctant to follow him was plain, and the cause of her reluctance became all too apparent the moment she stepped on the scales. 'Good grief, Mary, you've put on another three kilos since I weighed you last month!'

'I really don't see how I can,' she replied, all wide-eyed innocence. 'Maybe I'm wearing heavier shoes…'

'Mary, you'd have to be wearing cement boots to make that much of a difference,' he protested. 'You were twenty-one kilos overweight last month, and now you're almost twenty-four kilos over the recommended weight for your height.'

'I like my food, Doctor, always have.'

'And as I explained to you before, any excess weight

you carry is putting an increased strain on your heart, along
with your bronchitis,' he said, striving for calm. 'Have you
at least stopped smoking?'

'Oh, yes, Doctor.' His eyebrows lifted and Mary
Cassidy's florid face became even more flushed. 'Well
maybe sometimes I have one or two when I'm nervous or
upset.'

'One or two?'

She tried to meet his eyes, and failed. 'Perhaps it's nearer
four or five…'

'And perhaps you're still on forty a day,' he groaned.
'Mary, you have chronic bronchitis, a disease that's narrowing and obstructing the airways of your lungs. Your
constant cough is a clear indication that your lungs are
damaged. If you don't stop smoking and lose weight,
you're going to develop emphysema, then pulmonary hypertension, and you'll really be in trouble.'

'I thought you said the inhaler would cure me,' she said
defensively.

'I said it would *help* your symptoms, but you have to
help yourself. Use the bronchodilator regularly, lose weight
and *stop smoking*!'

She gazed at him silently for a moment, then tried a
conciliatory smile. 'I don't suppose there's an easier way,
is there?'

'Mary—'

'Only joking, Doctor,' she said, beaming, but he had the
depressing suspicion she wasn't.

In a month's time she'd probably be still overweight, still
smoking and still denying the inevitable. The only difference would be that she'd be even closer to developing pulmonary hypertension and eventually heart failure.

'I'll make you out another prescription for some more of
the bronchodilator,' he said, sitting down in defeat at his
desk and reaching for his pad. 'Try to use it regularly. It
isn't a cure, but it will help.'

'Talking of helping, Doctor,' she commented as he tore the prescription off his pad and handed it to her, 'my sister told me you were absolutely wonderful at Maeshowe on Sunday with Mrs Wallace. Saved the woman's life, Jean said.'

Michael groaned inwardly. He'd forgotten that Mary Cassidy was Jean Mackay's sister, and if Jean could have taken a degree in local gossip, Mary could have romped home with a doctorate.

'I did no more than my job,' he replied. 'Now, if there's nothing else…'

'Jean said…' Mary paused and flicked a non-existent speck of dust from her sleeve. Here it comes, Michael thought with a sinking heart. Here comes the inquisition. 'Jean told me Mrs Seton and her children were with you at Maeshowe.'

'Her car was out of commission,' Michael said, his voice casual, dismissive. 'Her son was really keen to see the tomb, so naturally I offered to take them.'

'Oh, naturally.' Mary nodded, her small brown eyes irritatingly knowing. 'And did you enjoy your day out before poor Mrs Wallace became ill?'

He had. In fact, if anybody had told him he could have had so much fun with a six-year-old and a ten-year-old in tow he would have said they needed their heads examined, but he'd enjoyed every minute of it until he and Bethany had been left alone at Maeshowe. Until he'd kissed her and she'd stared at him in absolute horror.

'It was a very pleasant day,' he declared quickly, suddenly realising from Mary's appraising gaze that he'd waited far too long to answer her. 'Now, as I said, if there's nothing else…'

'Do I take it we might be hearing wedding bells soon, Doctor?' she asked coyly.

'Certainly not,' he snapped. 'Mrs Seton and I… we're…we…' Oh, damn, he could feel himself blushing

and, judging from Mary's gleeful expression, she could see
it. 'Mrs Cassidy—'

'Jean said you and Mrs Seton seem to be good friends.
*Very* good friends.'

'That's because we are,' Michael retorted. Or at least he
hoped they still were after that kiss. 'And now you really
must excuse me,' he added, getting to his feet and striding
to the door. 'I'll see you in a month's time, and remember
what I said. Use the inhaler, lose weight and stop smoking.'

'Yes, but—'

'Goodbye, Mrs Cassidy,' he said, throwing open the door
pointedly.

She went with ill-concealed bad grace and he couldn't
stop himself from slamming the door shut behind her,
though he knew his action would simply add fuel to her
speculation. But, dammit, he'd had to endure his sister's
inquisition for the past five days, so why the hell should
he have to put up with a patient grilling him as well?

Because you asked for it, a little voice at the back of his
mind pointed out as he walked back to his desk and threw
himself into his chair. You know what small communities
are like, and you should have realised there was bound to
be gossip, especially as you haven't been out with anyone
for two years.

There would have been considerably more gossip if anyone had seen you kissing Bethany, he thought grimly, and
he still didn't know why he'd done it, except that she'd
looked so damned appealing, her huge grey eyes softly luminous in the darkness, her lips half-parted and moist.

A groan came from him as his body reacted with unbri-
dled enthusiasm to the memory he'd just conjured up, and
swiftly he reached for the phone, only to put it down again
as he'd done so many times over the last few days. He had
to talk to her—he knew he did—but what could he say—
'Hi, Bethany, it's Michael, and I'm just phoning to repeat

how sorry I am about kissing you but it was a joke, a temporary aberration, an act of insanity'?

She wouldn't believe it—he didn't believe it—but he knew he had to do something soon or he would lose her friendship altogether. And he didn't want to lose it. He wanted to keep seeing her. Seeing her smile, hearing her laughter, watching the way her hair kept threatening to descend to her shoulders and never quite making it.

It's called involvement, the annoying little voice at the back of his mind pointed out, and unconsciously he shook his head. It was called sexual deprivation. Actually, a mega case of sexual deprivation if the dreams he'd been having since Sunday were anything to go by. He didn't want to get involved with a woman with two kids, and she quite obviously didn't want to get involved with him, but he did want to keep her friendship, so the only sensible thing they could do was to try to forget what had happened and go back to being just good friends.

'Mrs Mackintosh to see you if you're ready, Doctor,' his receptionist announced over the intercom.

He groaned out loud. Daisy Mackintosh. Jean Mackay's best friend and bosom pal. Well, he didn't need two guesses to figure out what she was doing in his surgery.

With a deep sigh he leant forward and pressed the intercom button. Bethany didn't know how lucky she was. As an incomer, at least she didn't have to face an inquisition about her actions, whereas he... He had a horrible feeling he'd be lucky if he got through the rest of the day without hitting someone.

'I didn't know you and Dr Harcus were dating, Bethany?'

'We're not dating.'

'But I heard— Somebody told me—'

'Could you turn over for me, Linda, so I can begin massaging your back and shoulders?' Bethany interrupted swiftly before the girl could say anything else. Before she could begin asking the same questions everybody else had been asking for the last five days.

Questions like 'So, when did you and Dr Harcus become an item, then?', and 'Is it serious?'

Why, oh, why had she ever gone to Maeshowe? If she and the children had come straight home after Skara Brae no one would have seen them with Michael and there would have been none of this endless speculation and gossip. And if you'd hadn't gone to Maeshowe, her mind pointed out, Elsie Wallace would be dead, instead of recuperating in the Kirkwall Infirmary, and is that really what you want?

'Then it isn't true that you and Dr Harcus are getting married?' Linda murmured into the massage table.

Bethany all but dropped the mixture of thyme, rosemary, cypress and eucalyptus peppermint she was using to relax Linda Balfour's muscles. 'Of course it's not true! Where on earth did you hear that?'

'It's what everyone's saying in Kirkwall...'

'Then everyone's wrong,' Bethany said tightly. 'Dr Harcus and I are friends, that's all.'

Or at least they had been until...

No, she wasn't going to think about that kiss, she told herself, feeling her cheeks burn as she began massaging Linda's shoulders. All that kiss proved was that she was suffering from a bad case of sexual deprivation. Actually a mega case of sexual deprivation if the dreams she'd been having since Sunday were anything to go by.

'Are you feeling any better today, Linda?' she asked, forcing her mind back to the girl quickly.

'About the same really. I know if I don't take any exercise the stiffness in my joints will only get worse but it's a catch-22 situation. If I felt well enough to take some exercise I'd do it, but I can't do any exercise because I feel so ill.'

'Most CFS sufferers feel the same.' Bethany nodded.

'But if you can make yourself take even a short walk it will stimulate the release of endorphins, the body's natural painkillers.'

'I don't want to release my body's natural painkillers,' Linda retorted unexpectedly. 'I just want my life back. I'm only twenty-six years old, Bethany, and yet I walk like an old woman. Three years ago I could sail, swim, play tennis—'

'And you'll do it again—'

'Yes, but *when*?' Linda demanded, tears plain in her voice. 'I was always so fit, so healthy.'

'Fitness—or lack of it—doesn't seem to be a factor with chronic fatigue syndrome.' Bethany sighed. 'It can hit anyone at any time, be they a marathon runner or a slob. The only thing sufferers appear to have in common is that the illness generally started after either a viral infection like flu, or food poisoning, but why that should trigger the condition in some people and not in others is anybody's guess. Is the St John's wort I gave you helping at all?'

'A bit,' Linda conceded. 'I don't feel quite so anxious and tense all the time, but the skullcap you prescribed is giving me the most awful indigestion.'

Bethany frowned. 'We could try vervain. It works just as well on supporting your nervous system as skullcap, and with the gingko it will improve any impaired circulation in the brain, which seems to be implicated in some people with CFS. Are you still sure you're not pregnant?'

'Of course I'm not pregnant!' Linda retorted bitterly. 'I'd have to be insane to be trying for a baby right now!'

Gently Bethany placed her hands on the girl's shoulders. 'Linda, I have to ask. Some herbs can be harmful to a foetus, and even something as simple as liquorice can make you very ill indeed if you have high blood pressure or anaemia.'

For a moment Linda was silent, then she said in a very

small voice, 'I'm sorry. I didn't mean to snap at you but I'm so tired of feeling like this, so tired of *being* tired.'

And I don't know how I feel, Bethany thought as she poured more oil into the palms of her hands and tried to focus once more on her patient.

She hadn't seen Michael since Sunday and though part of her missed him, missed the way he always seemed able to cheer her up whenever she felt down, the other part—the major part—never wanted to see him again.

That's being chicken, her mind pointed out. OK, all right, so she was chicken, but when they met they were either going to have to talk about that kiss or spend the rest of their lives tiptoeing round one another, and she didn't want to talk about that kiss.

Her life was settled, organised and a lot happier than it had been for years. Yes, there were times when she was lonely—very lonely—but being lonely wasn't a good enough reason to risk being hurt again. Being lonely didn't mean she should get involved with a man who, by all accounts, was little more than a womaniser.

'I think it's a great shame you and Dr Harcus aren't dating,' Linda declared suddenly, as though she'd read her mind. 'In fact, I can't think of any other two people I know who would be better suited.'

'Linda—'

'I know—it's none of my business.' The girl chuckled. 'Sorry.'

Not half as sorry as I am, Bethany thought, desperately trying to swallow the large lump that had formed in her throat as she found herself remembering how horrified Michael had looked after he'd kissed her.

Why had he kissed her? Because she'd been there, because she'd seemed available, because he'd needed the practice? She didn't like any of the answers she was getting so the only thing she could do if she wanted to remain friends with him—and she did, despite what had happened at Maeshowe—was to try to forget what had happened. The only problem was—could she?

'Could you make me up some more of the echinacea?' Linda asked when Bethany had finished her massage. 'I think I've got enough until next week but—'

'You don't want to run out.' Bethany nodded. 'I'll make you up some vervain at the same time. Do you want to call by for it, or would you rather I put it in the post for you?'

'The post would be better. Today's one of my better days, but I don't know how I'll feel tomorrow.'

Bethany sighed as she watched the girl going out of her consulting room. Her herbs didn't seem to be making much of an improvement to Linda's condition but it was early days yet. She'd seen cases where it had taken months before there was any change. All she could hope for—for Linda's sake—was that it wouldn't be that long.

Quickly she washed her hands and sat down at her desk to update Linda's notes, but she'd only just started when her consulting-room door flew open and Mardi appeared.

'Bethany, I've just heard something really awful. Nora Linklater's collapsed and been taken to the Kirkwall Infirmary!'

Bethany stared at her in disbelief. 'But I just saw her three days ago and she said she was beginning to feel better.'

'I know. You don't think… I mean, it couldn't be something you've given her that's caused her to collapse, could it?'

'Of course not,' Bethany retorted angrily. 'Nothing I gave her could have made her ill.'

But she could have had a heart attack, or a stroke. During the menopause the levels of oestrogen and progesterone, which gave a woman some protection against those two potential killers, gradually decreased, and though Nora's blood pressure had been normal when she'd last taken it that didn't necessarily mean she was safe.

Quickly Bethany scanned her appointment book. Her next patient wasn't due until three o'clock. If she drove like the wind she could get to Kirkwall Infirmary and back before Mr Jarvis arrived.

'Where are you going?' Mardi asked in amazement as Bethany made for the door.

'To the Infirmary.'

'But—'

'Mardi, you know what hospitals are like. They won't tell me anything over the phone, especially as I'm not a relative, but they might give me some information if I'm standing on their doorstep.'

'But what about Mr Jarvis?' her receptionist protested.

'I'll be back before he gets here, and if I'm not, stall him.'

And before Mardi could protest any further she was out of the door and into her car and on her way to Kirkwall.

She might just as well have saved herself the petrol and the nervous strain she realised when she got to the hospital. The doctor on duty in A and E listened to her with a patronising air that made Bethany long to slap him, then said outright that he didn't consider her a doctor and he wasn't going to tell her anything.

She tried sweet reason, argument and even managed to dredge up what she hoped was a winning smile, but it didn't get her anywhere and she was on her way out, biting her lip with frustration, when she saw Anne Bichan walking ahead of her in the corridor—Anne Bichan who, she suddenly remembered, was a staff nurse in A and E.

'Bethany, I can't tell you anything,' Anne exclaimed in horror after she'd explained why she was there. 'Giving out details of a patient's condition to someone who isn't family or the patient's doctor—Lord, I'd be hauled up in front of the senior nursing officer if anyone found out!'

'I wouldn't tell anyone—I promise on my children's lives that I wouldn't tell anyone,' Bethany declared, 'but for my own peace of mind I'd like to know what's wrong with Nora—can't you see that?'

For a second Anne gazed at her uncertainly, then hustled her into one of A and E's private waiting rooms and shut the door.

'OK, now, you didn't hear a word of this from me, remember,' she began. 'Nora was brought in a couple of hours ago after one of her neighbours got a bit concerned when he couldn't get any reply to her doorbell. He rang for the police and when they broke in they found her unconscious on the floor.'

'A stroke—a heart attack?' Bethany queried, and Anne shook her head.

'The police found a pile of empty bottles in her bathroom with your name on them, and they think she took the lot.'

'You mean, they think she was trying to commit suicide?' Bethany gasped. 'But why should she? She—'

'Bethany, she wasn't trying to kill herself,' Anne interrupted. 'All she wanted was to make herself ill enough to be taken to hospital, and that's exactly what she did. We're pumping out her stomach now.'

'I'm sorry… I don't understand…'

'Nora has Munchausen's.'

Bethany gazed at her in horror. Munchausen's syndrome—the condition that caused people to go repeatedly to hospital or to various doctors with symptoms and signs which suggested serious illness. Patients could deliberately make themselves ill by swallowing blood, or by inserting needles into their chests, or—if they were really desperate to get into hospital—they could take carefully calculated overdoses.

'Didn't Dr Harcus tell you about her?' Anne asked, watching her not without sympathy.

'No, no, he didn't,' Bethany murmured.

'I guess he really couldn't,' Anne observed. 'I mean, patients' details are confidential so it's not the kind of thing he could broadcast without getting into trouble with the GMC.'

'Anne… Could you do me another huge favour and find out how she is now? I know I shouldn't ask,' she continued quickly as the girl groaned. 'You've already told me much more than you should have, but I'd be really grateful.'

'But—'

'Please, Anne?'

She sighed. 'All right, but this is my very last favour, Bethany, OK?'

It was the only one she needed, Bethany thought as she paced the waiting-room floor after Anne had gone, unable to relax.

Munchausen's syndrome. It had never occurred to her, not even for a moment. And to think she'd felt sorry for the woman, had even considered Michael an unsympathetic swine when Nora had told her he'd suggested she needed psychiatric counselling. No wonder he'd suggested counselling. If only she'd asked him why, but it was too late now for 'if onlys'.

Too late now for a lot of things, she thought with dismay as the door of the waiting room suddenly opened and Michael appeared.

That she was the last person he expected—or wanted—to see was clear. Well, the feeling was mutual, but one of them had to say something or they'd still be staring at one another in uncomfortable silence days from now.

'You're…you're looking well,' she offered. Actually, she thought he looked terrible, as though he hadn't slept for days.

'You're looking well, too,' he replied. She looked like hell, he thought grimly, like she was carrying all the worries of the world on her shoulders. 'Bethany—'

'I didn't know Nora Linklater suffered from Munchausen's.'

'I know.'

'Nothing I gave her would have harmed a normal person who'd followed my prescription,' she continued, determined that he should be in no doubt. 'Black cohosh, lemon balm, motherwort—they're all perfectly safe when taken in moderation.'

'Bethany, I'm not blaming you.' His voice was gentle, reassuring, and for a second she was thought he was going to take her hands in his, then he clearly decided against it. 'People like Nora Linklater... They're devious, cunning. They have to be to get what they want, which is constant medical attention.'

'She told me she was suffering very badly with the menopause.'

'That's a new one,' he observed dryly. 'When she first came to Orkney five years ago we had no idea she suffered from Munchausen's and had to find out the hard way. I've been trying to get her to accept psychiatric counselling but...' He shrugged and shook his head. 'If I blame anyone for this it's myself for not taking a more active interest in your patients.'

'Maybe you'd like me to give you a complete list of them?' she said, half-jokingly, and saw him nod. 'Michael, I couldn't do that. My patients have as much right to confidentiality as yours.'

She was right, he knew she was. She was also quite plainly as embarrassed as hell, and he knew it wasn't about Nora Linklater.

Get it over with, Michael, his mind urged. Say what you've got to say about that kiss, and get it over with.

'Bethany, I think we should talk—clear the air—about what happened at Maeshowe.'

She stiffened but didn't say anything, and a trickle of sweat ran down his back. Lord, let me get this right, he prayed. Don't let me make a mess of it or I'll lose her completely.

'Bethany, all I can repeat is that I'm sorry, and if I could turn back the clock I would, but I can't. I... Well, I'm not into commitment, involvement, and I know you don't want that either.' He hesitated, almost as though he was waiting for her to say something, then thrust his hand awkwardly through his golden brown hair. 'Look, I guess what I'm trying to say is I value our friendship too much to risk losing it, and I promise you it won't ever happen again.'

Still she said nothing, and he scanned her face uncertainly. 'That is what you want, isn't it?'

It was—of course it was—so why, she wondered, did she feel a quite irrational desire to burst into tears?

'Bethany?' He took a step towards her.

Instinctively she stepped back and saw his jaw tighten. 'Of course it's what I want, Michael,' she said with spurious brightness. 'You and I... I mean, we...' Her voice trailed away into silence under his watchful gaze and she stared up at him helplessly. Lord, but he was a handsome man, but Jake had been handsome, too, and at least he'd been attracted to her at the beginning.

Michael wasn't attracted to her. He'd just made it all too abundantly clear that all he wanted from her was friendship, but how could they go back to being friends when simply seeing him again was enough to make her lips tingle with the memory of that kiss? How could she be friends with a man who made her heart feel as though it were being squeezed in a vice and there wasn't enough air for her to breathe?

Look, if he can do it, you can, her mind urged. Good grief, you're not a teenager in the throes of your first crush. You're a divorcee of thirty-three with two children. So he kissed you—so what? Just because your whole world felt suddenly as though it had been tilted sideways, it doesn't mean you can't get over it.

'Michael—'

'Bethany, the good news about Nora—' Anne bit off the rest of what she'd been about to say with a horrified gasp as she came into the waiting room and saw Michael. 'Dr Harcus, I...I didn't know you were here. I...um...I...'

'It's my fault, Michael,' Bethany said quickly. 'I asked Anne to find out how Nora was. No one would tell me anything—'

'And how is she?' he interrupted. 'Strictly off the record, of course.'

Anne shot him a grateful glance. 'There's no sign of any liver, heart or kidney damage. She's going to feel pretty wretched for a couple of days but she'll make a full recovery.'

Bethany let out the breath she hadn't even known she'd been holding, and managed a weak smile. She'd got what she'd come for—the most accurate update on Nora's condition it was possible to have—and there was no point in her lingering.

'Wouldn't you like a cup of coffee before you go?' Anne suggested as Bethany pulled her car keys from her pocket and made for the door. 'You look pretty stressed out to me and the canteen here is pretty good.'

Bethany shook her head. 'I haven't time. I've a patient in forty minutes.'

'Even so—'

'I'll take care of her,' Michael said firmly, and a smile curved Anne's lips.

'I reckon you will at that,' she said, nodding.

'I don't need anyone to take care of me,' Bethany protested as Michael accompanied her down the corridor and out of the hospital. 'I'm fine.'

He ignored the patent lie. 'This business with Nora... I'll make sure it becomes known she has Munchausen's.'

She stopped in the centre of the path, aghast. 'Michael, you can't go around telling people that! She's one of your patients. It wouldn't be ethical—'

'Bethany, if I don't drop one or two hints in the right

ear, what do you think is going to happen to your business?'

'Nothing will happen to my business,' she retorted, 'but if you break a patient's confidentiality, you'll be in serious trouble.'

He thrust his hands through his hair, struggled to keep his temper and failed. 'For God's sake, woman, will you use the sense you were born with? Once people get over the shock of Nora collapsing they're going to start wondering *why* she collapsed. Nora sure as hell isn't going to tell anyone the truth when she gets out of hospital, and gradually people will remember she was consulting you. They'll put two and two together, come up with five and decide that what you prescribe is dangerous. It will ruin you, Bethany.'

He was right. The very first thing her own receptionist had asked was whether Nora's collapse might have been due to something Bethany had given her, but she couldn't accept his help. Not only would it be unethical for him to do what he was suggesting, she was already relying on him too much already, and if she was to have any hope of retaining her own strength, she had to start distancing herself from him—and fast.

'Michael, you mean well, I know you do, but I have to deal with this in my own way.'

Was ever a man damned with such faint praise? he thought ruefully. 'Bethany, listen to me—'

'No, you listen,' she interrupted. 'You said we were friends, so as a friend, please, understand that I have to live my own life, do what I think is best.'

'But, Bethany—' She was already walking towards her car, and he had to quicken his pace to catch up. 'Look, why don't I drop by tomorrow and we can discuss this properly?'

'I'm sorry, but I'm fully booked tomorrow,' she lied as she opened the car door.

'Tomorrow evening, then?' he pressed.

Have him in the house with no patient to use as an excuse to get away? No way, not now. Ye gods, just the thought was enough to make her pulses race. 'I'm sorry, Michael, but I can't. I...I have plans for tomorrow night.'

'What about the day after, then?' he asked as she got into her car and started the engine.

He didn't hear her reply but somehow he didn't think it was, 'I'll look forward to seeing you.' She drove off at speed, and a deep sigh came from him as he gazed after her disappearing car.

When he'd been eight or nine he'd asked his father how he'd know when he'd met the woman he wanted to marry, and his father had just smiled and said, 'You'll know.' It hadn't satisfied him then, and it hadn't satisfied him when he'd been growing up, but now...

He'd told Bethany he didn't want to get involved, that he didn't want commitment—but he'd lied. The second he'd seen her again he'd known that all his talk about not wanting to get involved with a divorced woman with kids was a sham. A sham he'd dreamt up because he was frightened. Frightened she'd be appalled if he suggested it, frightened she'd knock him back, frightened that if he pushed too hard she might disappear as Lorraine had done.

And Lorraine at least had lived with him for a year before she'd decided she'd had enough, whereas nothing about the way Bethany looked at him, or behaved in his company, suggested she felt anything but friendship for him. Indeed, there were times when he wondered if she even saw him as a man at all, and yet he...

He hadn't made love to her—good grief, he'd only kissed her once and that all too briefly—but he knew. This was the woman he wanted to spend the rest of his life with. This was the woman he wanted to have, and to hold, from this day forward, but for the first time in his life he was completely out of his depth. For the first time in his life he didn't have a clue how he was going to get her.

# CHAPTER SEVEN

'WE'VE only had five cancellations this week, Bethany,' Mardi said, her plump face encouraging. 'Perhaps things are beginning to look up.'

And pigs might fly, Bethany thought miserably, but managed a smile. 'Has Connie Robson arrived yet?'

Her receptionist shook her head. 'Her appointment isn't until three o'clock, and it's not quite three yet. She won't let you down, Bethany.'

No, Connie wouldn't let her down. She was a good friend and a loyal one, but one loyal friend wasn't going to make up for all the other people who had cancelled their appointments over the last three weeks. One loyal friend wasn't going to pay the bills accumulating on her desk.

You should have let Michael help you, her mind whispered as she walked through to her consulting room and stared bleakly out of the window at the golden corn in the fields beside the house and the high, wispy clouds which showed autumn was fast approaching. One word from him and you wouldn't be in this mess.

Yes, and if anybody found out that he'd dropped that one word, it wouldn't just be my business on the line, but his career as well.

If she was sensible she'd cut her losses, sell the cottage and go back to Winchester. But being sensible meant uprooting the children and herself all over again. It meant leaving behind the friends she'd made since she'd come to Orkney. And it would mean never seeing Michael again.

Stop it, Bethany, she told herself as her throat clogged with unshed tears. You don't want a relationship, remem-

114

ber? You're happy as you are, remember? But she wasn't happy, and she knew she wasn't.

Connie was.

'No, I'm not pregnant yet,' she replied in answer to Bethany's query when she bounced into the consulting room, looking suntanned and fit. 'I just haven't felt this good in years. It must be the agnus castus you gave me— or maybe it's the rose oil. It's certainly done wonders for my sex life!'

Bethany's eyebrows rose. 'Really?'

'You bet. Simon loves the smell, and it makes him very...' Connie dimpled. 'Well, you know!'

Bethany wished she did. Maybe if she used a whole tanker-load of the stuff Michael might get interested. Maybe if she bathed in it night and day he would stop seeing her as a friend and start seeing her as...

And she was doing it again, she realised. Thinking about him, fantasising about him, and for what?

He wasn't interested in her. She was plain and fat and dull, and even if she'd been gorgeous and scintillating he'd only be interested in her for a brief affair—and was that really what she wanted? Actually, yes, she thought with a deep sigh, right now, yes, that was exactly what she wanted.

'Talking about Michael...'

Had they been? Bethany couldn't for the life of her remember. 'What about Michael?' she asked casually.

'Mardi told me you haven't seen him for ages.'

Bethany managed a small, tight smile. She was going to kill her receptionist—kill her, then plead temporary insanity. 'There's no need for me to see him, Connie. I have all the details I need for Linda Balfour—'

'I wasn't thinking about Linda Balfour.'

Connie's gaze was hopeful, speculative, and Bethany sighed. 'Connie, I know you love your brother dearly, and

there's nothing you'd like better than to see him walk down
the aisle with somebody—'

'Not just *somebody*…'

'But it isn't going to be with me.'

'Bethany—'

'You'll be needing more agnus castus, I expect. If you
could come back tomorrow I should have it ready for you,
and I'd also like you to try adding peppermint oil to your
bath. It will act as a tonic, increasing the circulation to your
organs.'

Connie pouted. 'You're hopeless, you know that, don't
you? Good grief, if a man as good-looking as Michael was
interested in me I wouldn't be running away.'

Interested in her? In a pig's eye he was interested in her.
If he'd been interested he'd have dropped by. If he'd been
interested he'd have lifted the phone to talk to her, but it
had been three weeks since she'd seen him. Three long,
interminable weeks.

Quickly she picked up her notebook. 'Connie, I don't
want to be rude, but I'm pretty busy this morning, so if
there's nothing else…?'

Michael's sister shook her head and sighed. 'I don't
know who's worse—you or Michael.'

'I think we just both know what we want, and it isn't
one another.' Bethany couldn't help but laugh as she accompanied Connie to the front door, but her laughter died
when she opened it and saw Michael standing on the
threshold.

'Is that so?' Connie commented, glancing slyly from her
to Michael, then back again, her eyes taking in the betraying flush of colour on Bethany's cheeks and the even darker
hue on Michael's. 'Well, pardon me if I say hogwash.'

'Connie—'

'I'm going—I'm going.' She smiled as Bethany gazed
at her in consternation. 'Take care of yourself—you, too,

Michael. I'll drop by tomorrow to pick up the agnus cas-
us.'

'Agnus castus?' Michael repeated, his gaze sharpening
s his sister drove away. 'You're treating Connie, aren't
ou? Oh, Bethany—'

'Michael, before you say anything, I can't discuss a pa-
ent with you.'

'You don't need to,' he declared, his voice tight. 'I know
ery well why Connie's seeing you, and I want you to tell
er to stop.'

Her jaw dropped. 'I'll do no such thing.'

'Bethany, this is my sister we're talking about—'

'And it doesn't occur to you that I might actually be able
 help her? No, it obviously doesn't,' she continued acidly
hen he opened his mouth, then closed it again, 'because
ou still think my profession is little better than glorified
umbo-jumbo.'

A deep tide of colour darkened his cheeks. 'Bethany—'

'I can treat Linda Balfour so long as you practically sit
 my consulting room with me,' she continued inexorably,
ut when it comes to treating your sister all your old prej-
dices come racing back to the surface.'

'Bethany, I'm a doctor,' he protested. 'A professional—'

'And I'm still a quack, right?' she interrupted, her face
old.

'Bethany, listen—'

'I have neither the time nor the inclination. I've a patient
aiting.'

'Bethany, wait—'

But she didn't. She simply swung round and slammed
e front door shut, leaving him staring at it.

For a second he considered going in after her, then with
 muttered oath he whirled round and strode angrily down
e path.

He hadn't been to Sorrel Cottage for three weeks—three
eeks which had felt like an eternity—but he'd thought

he'd give her time to calm down, time to see he'd bee
right about Nora Linklater. And what had he discovered th
minute he'd got here? That she was treating his sister.

Connie had been examined by some of the best brain
in the country and they'd all said the same thing. That
was highly unlikely she would ever have a child and it wa
wrong of Bethany to raise her hopes, to imply that with
few herbs she could achieve what all the experts couldn'

And the experts are always right, are they? a little voic
demanded in his mind. They don't ever get it wrong, mak
mistakes?

Of course they made mistakes, but they were traine
They had years of study and expertise to draw on, ar
Bethany…

Was right, he suddenly realised with a groan. He we
prejudiced. Prejudiced, and narrow-minded, and blinkere

'Michael, wait for me!'

He turned, startled, to see Katie hurtling round the si
of the house towards him, and just got his arms up in tim
to catch her.

'You were going away without seeing me!' she pr
tested.

'As if I would,' he replied, forcing a smile to his lip
'How's my favourite girl?'

'We haven't seen you for ages and ages and, o
Michael, I have missed you.'

Michael gazed down into her open, shining face and h
heart contracted. It wasn't just Bethany he'd missed, h
realised. It was her children as well.

He'd missed talking to them, listening to them. He
missed the trusting way they gazed up at him, so sure
their innocence that he could fix anything. It made him fe
ten feet tall. It made him feel needed. It made him fe
whole.

'And I…I've missed you,' he murmured huskily, h
throat almost closing with emotion.

'Why don't you come round any more?' Katie asked, her small face troubled. 'I thought we were friends.'

'We are, sweetheart,' he replied, all too conscious of the solid lump that seemed wedged in his throat. 'But I've been busy—'

'Mummy's thinking of going back to Winchester, and I don't want to go. I like it here.'

His brows drew together. 'She told you this?'

Katie shook her head. 'I heard her talking to Grandma on the phone. Something about things not being very good since somebody called Nora got sick.'

She hadn't given it enough time, he thought angrily. Of course things weren't good, and they wouldn't get any better unless she let him help her. Well, he was through standing on the sidelines. He was going to help her whether she liked it or not.

'Katie, I need to talk to your mum,' he said, putting her down quickly.

'And then will you come back and play with me?' she asked, her large grey eyes fixed entreatingly on him.

'You bet, but right now…right now I have something very important to say to your mum.'

Determinedly he walked into the cottage, but Mardi shook her head when he asked if Bethany was free.

'Not for another forty minutes, Dr Harcus. She's giving someone a massage, and she's only just start—'

A resounding crash from the consulting room, followed by the all-too-clear sound of Bethany's angry, raised voice, had them both whirling round to stare at the closed door with varying degrees of shock.

'Who's she got in there?' Michael demanded.

'Ralph Elliot—'

Michael didn't wait to hear any more. Before Mardi could prevent him, he'd thrown open the door to find Bethany standing on one side of the massage table, her cheeks flushed, several buttons on her tunic top undone, and Ralph, clad only in a towel, looking frustrated and fu rious.

'Michael, it's all right,' Bethany said, catching hold o the back of his shirt as he advanced on the accountan grimly, having clearly taken in the situation in a glance. ' can handle it.'

'Not this low-life, you can't,' he replied, his eyes fixe on Ralph. 'This low-life needs a lesson in manners.'

'Michael, please—'

She might just as well have saved her breath. H shrugged out of her grasp, ignoring the ripping sound from somewhere around his collar, and bore down on Ralph wh backed away, one hand in the air in a gesture of appeal the other clutching his towel desperately to his waist.

'Michael, it's not how it looks,' the accountant declare placatingly. 'We were only having a little fun.'

'*Fun?*' Michael repeated, his jaw tight. 'It doesn't loo to me as though the lady was having *fun*. It looks to me a though the lady is due one very big apology.'

'For what?' Ralph asked unwisely. 'Everybody know that massage is simply a polite euphemism for somethin a whole lot more interesting. If the stupid bitch—'

The rest of what Ralph had been about to say ended i a high-pitched squeak as he suddenly found himself lifte off his feet.

'You will apologise to this lady, and you will apologis now,' Michael declared, each word like a whiplash. 'The you will get out and never come back. And if I hear on word…' He lifted Ralph higher until his feet were almo a foot off the floor. 'If I hear so much as a *whisper* sur rounding this lady's good name I will come round to you office and beat you to a pulp. *Understand?*'

Ralph nodded frantically, and to Bethany's surpris Michael put him down. But he wasn't finished with th accountant yet.

'You're trying my patience, Ralph,' he said after the man
d mumbled out his apology. 'I said you were to get out.'
The accountant looked at him in horror. 'You can't ex-
ct me to leave here wearing only a towel?'

'Can't I?' Michael glanced down at his watch. 'You have
e seconds, Ralph.'

'But—'

'Four seconds, Ralph.'

The accountant took one look at Michael's face and fled,
aving Bethany staring up at Michael, not knowing
hether she wanted to laugh or cry. After a brief consid-
ation, she opted for being defensive.

'There was no need for you to do that,' she declared,
ishing her knees would stop shaking. 'I had everything
der control.'

He gazed pointedly at the expanse of plain white cotton
a she was revealing, and nodded wryly. 'So I see.'

Mortified, she did up her buttons as quickly as she could,
en bit her lip. 'I…I suppose I ought to say thank you.'

He shrugged. 'Rescuing damsels in distress is my spe-
ality. Hey, are you OK?' he added with concern as she
ddenly sat down on the massage table.

'Just a little bit wobbly,' she admitted.

'That settles it,' he declared. 'You're coming to my place
r dinner tonight.'

She stared at him, stunned. 'I can't—'

'Bethany, you've had a very bad fright and a night out
ill do you good. Get Mardi to babysit, and I'll expect you
eight.'

'But—'

'No excuses, no refusals, Bethany,' he said firmly. 'I
ant you on my doorstep tonight at eight sharp, and if
ou're not there I'll come and collect you.'

And without waiting for her reply he strode out of the
or, leaving her gazing, open-mouthed, after him.

'Well, is he masterful or what?' Mardi exclaimed in ad-

miration as she came into the consulting room, clearly ha
ing heard every word. 'I can babysit for you tonight,
bother.'

There was obviously no point in arguing. Between Ma
and Michael her evening appeared to have been well a
truly organised, and Bethany gave in with ill-concealed b
grace. 'I won't be late back, I promise.'

'That's what you think,' her receptionist declared, h
eyes dancing. 'But once he's got you there—the candle
dinner for two, the soft music... I'd take along my too
brush if I were you, and my sexiest nightdress.'

A deep flush of crimson colour flooded across Bethany
cheeks. 'How many times do I have to tell you that Micha
and I are just friends?' she protested.

'That's the trouble,' Mardi said shrewdly. 'Ever hea
the saying, "Methinks the lady doth protest too much"'

Bethany had, and she didn't much like Mardi's infe
ence—especially as she had an uncomfortable feeling th
it was true.

'If the lady protests a lot, it's because the lady's sick
death of all this innuendo,' she said stiffly.

'Yeah, right.' Her receptionist winked as she went o
of the consulting room. 'I'll believe you, thousar
wouldn't.'

Bethany didn't care two hoots about the thousands, ju
the population of Orkney in general and Michael in part
ular.

She must have been out of her mind to have agreed
have dinner with him, she thought vexedly. Not that s
actually *had* agreed, she recalled. Well, it was done n
and she couldn't undo it, and having dinner with Micha
at his place, was no big deal. It would simply be a case
two professional friends sharing a meal, talking about m
tual patients. She could handle it. She could. She wo
have to.

*     *     *

Michael smiled a little ruefully as he gazed at his reflection in the bathroom mirror. Lord, he hadn't felt this nervous since the first time he'd asked a girl out, and that was more years ago now than he cared to remember.

He'd showered twice, changed his clothes twice, picked up the phone to tell Bethany something had come up— It had, in fact, in the shower when he'd found himself thinking about the way she'd looked at Maeshowe, her cheeks flushed, her lips slightly parted.

Hell, something had just come up again, he realised, wishing he'd put on looser trousers. He still had time to change, but into what? If he was too dressy and she came casual, she'd be uncomfortable. If he was too casual and she came in her best clothes…

At least the food was uncontroversial, he decided as he went into the kitchen to check on the progress of the lamb casserole. He knew she wasn't a vegetarian so there was nothing she could object to there, and the cheesecake to follow would surely be safe enough.

He glanced at the kitchen clock. Five minutes and she'd be here. Quickly he walked back to the sitting room. The candles on the dining table waiting to be lit, the flowers, the romantic music playing on the stereo. It looked…

Crass, he thought with a groan. Crass, and obvious and tacky. Like one of those sets in a fifties film when the hero was trying to seduce the heroine.

Ruthlessly he removed the candles from the table, and hit the 'off' button on the stereo just as he heard his front doorbell ring. Seduction wasn't what he had in mind for Bethany Seton. He wanted her to come into his arms willingly, to make love with him willingly, and for that love to last.

'Am I too early?' she asked when he opened the door, her gaze taking in his flustered appearance.

'Of course not.' He beamed, thanking his lucky stars he'd opted to wear a pair of smart casual trousers and a green shirt. Bethany's plain cream silk blouse and blue floral skirt might be understated but they were by no means casual. 'Come through to the sitting room.'

'You have a lovely home,' she observed, gazing admiringly at the beautiful collection of Chinese jade ornaments on a side table and the gleaming oak furniture that shrieked of money and antiquity.

'I'm glad you like it,' he said with a smile. 'You must bring the children some time for tea.'

He had to be kidding. She'd spend the whole time mentally biting her fingernails, waiting for the sound of breaking china or splintering wood.

'I made lamb casserole for dinner—I hope that's OK?' he continued as she sat down.

'Sounds lovely.'

'It shouldn't be very long—ten minutes tops.'

She smiled—a small, nervous smile that had him clenching his hands together against the impulse to stride across the room and take her in his arms and kiss her.

Slow down, he told himself, slow down. Getting her to accept she can trust you isn't going to be easy. Getting her to believe a man with your reputation can be serious isn't going to happen overnight. She'd been badly hurt by her ex and it's going to take time, but you've got all the time in the world, so go easy, take it slow.

'Bethany—'

'Michael—'

They'd spoken in unison and they both laughed a little nervously.

'I just wondered if you'd like a drink?' he said.

'Orange and soda would be nice,' she answered. 'I'd better not drink anything else as I'm driving.'

And I wish I hadn't come, she thought as he poured out their drinks. She glanced surreptitiously at her watch. How long would she have to stay before she could decently make her excuses? An hour and a half—two hours? Two hours

awkward silences, averted glances and stilted conversa-
on. It was going to be a nightmare.

'Did you know that smuggling was Orkney's most prof-
ible trade during the eighteenth and nineteenth centuries?'
ichael suddenly said. 'Everybody joined in. Churches
used the smuggled spirits, babies had supplies hidden in
eir cots, and as late as the 1860s you could buy smuggled
n over the counter of a Kirkwall bank.'

'You're making that up,' she protested, starting to laugh.

'It's as true as I'm standing here,' he insisted as he held
ut her drink, then his lips curved. 'And it made you smile.'
ne stiffened slightly and he sat down opposite her, his
ands on his knees. 'Bethany, the only reason I asked you
re tonight was because I thought you might welcome a
ance to relax after that unpleasantness this afternoon. No
rings, no hidden agenda, OK?'

Of course there were no strings, she told herself crossly.
ne was overreacting again, just as she always seemed to
verreact now whenever he was near.

'Will it hurt you much—financially, I mean—not having
alph as a patient any more?' he continued.

'What's one more amongst so many?' she replied with-
ut thinking, and saw his eyes darken with concern.

'Are things very bad at the moment?'

'Nothing I can't cope with,' she said lightly, wishing
e'd watched her tongue.

'Bethany, why won't you let me help you? If I dropped
word in the right ear—my big-mouth sister would be
rfect—'

'About your sister, Michael.' Take the bull by the horns,
e told herself. Get it out into the open. 'I can't, and I
on't stop treating her.'

'I don't want you to.'

'I might be able to help her, and— *You what?*'

He smiled at her, a little shamefaced. 'You were right
hen you said I was narrow-minded and prejudiced.'

'I didn't say that—'

'No, but it's true. I still have reservations about yo profession—I can't deny it—but that doesn't mean I shou prevent my sister from having treatment that might he her. And speaking of helping—'

'Michael, I won't let you endanger your career simp to help me out of a mess.'

'Bethany—'

'I think that's your oven timer,' she pointed out as bleeping sound came from the kitchen. 'The casserole mi be ready.'

It wasn't a very subtle way of telling him to butt out her life but, then, neither did he think there was any po in telling her that he had no intention of obeying her. She had three weeks to see sense, and she hadn't. Tomorro morning he was going to have a chat with his sister whetl Bethany liked it or not.

'That was a lovely meal,' Bethany said some time la when they'd made short work of the lamb casserole a the cheesecake. 'My ex didn't even know how to use a opener.'

'What does he do for a living?' he asked, more to ke her talking than with any great desire to know.

'You mean, you haven't heard of his TV programme *Around with Seton*?'

'I don't watch much TV,' he apologised. 'Golfing expe is he?'

A gurgle of laughter came from her. 'My ex would lo you. He has his own late night chat show, interviewing fi stars and people from the music business. It's very pop lar.'

And undoubtedly very well paid, he thought grimly, t he'd stake his career that Bethany never saw a penny. 'Hc did you meet?'

'You mean, how did someone as dull and ordinary

...e end up in the company of a TV personality?' she asked, ...miling.

'That isn't what I meant at all,' he protested. 'I meant—'

'We met at a party,' she continued, deciding to let him ...ff the hook. 'I'd just graduated and some friends took me ...o this really posh affair in Knightsbridge. I took one look ...t him and...' She smiled, remembering. 'I thought he was ...o handsome, and when I heard him talking about people ...d only ever read about—calling them by their first ...ames...' She shook her head. 'Sometimes I wonder what ...e ever saw in me.'

'I don't.'

'You mean it was probably very flattering to his ego to ...ave someone as naïve as I was at twenty-one, gazing ad...iringly up at him?' She laughed. 'You're probably right.'

He hadn't meant that—he hadn't meant that at all—and ...e was about to tell her so when she suddenly chuckled.

'What is it?' he asked curiously, his own lips curving in ...esponse. 'What's funny?'

She flushed adorably. 'Just something Mardi said this ...fternoon.'

'What did she say?'

She shook her head. 'Something silly—forget it.'

'If you think you can get away with that, then you don't ...now me,' he said, his smile widening. 'Come on—tell ...e.'

Her blush grew. 'She said...she actually warned me ...bout you. Said you might try to seduce me tonight.'

The smile on his face became fixed. 'And what did you ...ay to her?' he asked, deliberately casual.

'That she was talking nonsense, of course. You and I are ...iends.'

Tell her, his brain urged. She's just given you the perfect ...pportunity to tell her how you feel, so tell her now that ...e last thing you see her as is a friend, a chum, a pal. Tell

her you're falling in love with her—you *are* in love wit
her.

'Bethany—' The phone rang and he ignored it. 'Wh
Mardi said about us being friends… We are friends, o
course, but—'

'Shouldn't you answer that?' she interrupted, glancin
across at his mobile. 'It might be an emergency.'

'I'm not on call tonight—Simon is. Bethany, about wh
Mardi said—'

'But what if something big has happened—somethin
Simon can't handle on his own?'

Frankly, Michael didn't care if the entire population o
Orkney had suddenly been struck down by some appallin
debilitating disease, but he knew that if he didn't answe
the phone she'd never let it rest.

Irritably he went to retrieve it, heartily wishing th
Alexander Graham Bell had never been born, but after he
listened for a few seconds he turned to her. 'It's for you

'Me?' She stared at him in surprise, then a flash of alar
crossed her face. 'The children…'

'It isn't them. It's a man—he wouldn't give his name.

'But I don't know any men.'

She didn't know any men? What the hell was he, then—
some kind of eunuch? He held out the phone to her. 'I
get the coffee—give you some privacy.'

And while I'm in the kitchen I can try and get my hea
together, he thought as he strode out of the room withou
a backward glance.

How could she be so blind to his feelings? he wondere
as he poured some coffee into two cups and threw som
pieces of shortbread onto a plate, no longer caring wheth
it looked appetising or not. Maybe he should just drag he
into his arms and kiss her senseless. Yeah, right, a littl
voice at the back of his mind retorted. And when she slap
your face, what then?

Patience, Michael, he told himself, struggling to contr

is frustration. You've all the time in the world. But all
noughts of being patient vanished from his mind when he
arried the coffee into the sitting room and found her sitting
ost in thought.

'Something wrong?' he said with concern.

'It all depends on your perspective,' she murmured.
That was Jake. My ex-husband.'

Quickly he scanned her face, but he could read nothing
rom her expression, nothing at all. Take it calmly, he told
imself. Don't overreact. It could mean nothing, or...

'How did he know you were here?' he asked, putting
own the two coffees and moving the vase of flowers to
nake room for the shortbread.

'He got my number from a friend of mine in Winchester,
nd when he rang Sorrel Cottage Mardi told him I was
aving dinner with you. He wants...' Bethany paused. 'He
vants to come and see the children.'

One of the flowers in the vase was dying, he noticed. Its
ead was drooping, its petals browning at the edges. 'Are
ou going to let him?'

She shrugged. 'I don't really see how I can say no. He
s the children's father after all.'

It's taken him a hell of a long time to remember that,
Michael thought furiously. Tell him where to get off,
Bethany. Tell him you and the children have managed per-
ectly well—OK, reasonably well—for the last five years
vithout him, and he's got a bloody nerve to waltz back into
our life now.

But he didn't say that.

'When does he want to come?' he said instead, trying—
nd failing—to keep the edge out of his voice.

'A week on Friday. He said he'd like to spend a few
lays with the children.'

Don't overreact, Michael told himself, crushing down the
ngry retort that sprang to his lips. The last thing she
vants—or needs—at the moment is you screaming at her

like a maniac, saying her ex is a scumbag. 'Let's hope th[i]
good weather lasts for him, then,' he commented.

Was that all he was going to say? she wondered as sh[e]
stared across at him. That he hoped Jake got good weather[.]
She'd hoped… Stupidly, she'd half hoped that he might b[e]
angry, might tell her Jake had no part in either her or th[e]
children's lives any more, but, then, why should he?

Only she had this stupid fantasy about him. Only sh[e]
kept having this same silly dream that one day he migh[t]
turn, take her in his arms, and…

Abruptly she got to her feet. 'I have to go. I promise[d]
Mardi I wouldn't be late and it's almost ten o'clock now[.]

He gazed down at her impotently, seeing the strain i[n]
her large grey eyes, the weariness in her face. Lord, but h[e]
wanted to take her in his arms, to tell her he'd make ev[-]
erything all right, but it didn't seem like the right time s[o]
all he said was, 'Drive carefully, Bethany.'

And she did, through the rolling countryside, past th[e]
cheery lights of the houses dotting the Orkney landscape[,]
forcing herself not to think, forcing back the stupid, poin[t]
less tears that kept welling in her throat.

Mardi was all agog, of course, wanting to know how th[e]
evening had gone, but she pleaded tiredness and her recep[-]
tionist went away with a look of puzzled concern on he[r]
face.

Alistair was fast asleep but Katie had woken at the soun[d]
of her car and had to be settled down again with a drin[k]
and a story.

'Did you have a nice dinner with Michael?' she aske[d]
as Bethany tucked her in.

'Very nice, thanks. Now, cuddle down, sweetheart, it'[s]
late.'

Katie nodded and Bethany had got halfway to the doo[r]
when her daughter stopped her in her tracks.

'Mummy, do you think Alistair and I will ever have [a]

daddy? I mean a real daddy—somebody who stays with us all the time?'

Now, where in the world had that come from? Bethany wondered as she turned and gazed at her daughter's pensive face with dismay. Katie had never mentioned wanting a father before—had never even expressed an interest in her own father.

'I don't know,' she managed to reply. 'We'd have to find somebody we all liked. You, and me, and Alistair—'

'I like Michael.'

Oh, hellfire and damnation. She didn't need this, not now, not tonight. 'He's certainly a nice man, Katie—'

'No, I mean, I really, *really* like him, Mummy, and I think Alistair likes him, too.'

Katie's eyes were fixed on her, innocent, guileless, but it was plain what she was thinking. Two out of three was a majority decision. Actually, they could make it unanimous if Bethany was honest with herself, but tonight wasn't the night for honesty.

'That's nice to hear, sweetheart,' she declared evasively, 'but you really must cuddle down now. Mummy has a long day ahead of her tomorrow.'

And the day after that, and the day after that, she thought wearily as she switched off the light, leaving the door slightly ajar in case Katie had one of her bad dreams.

Why had she ever come to Orkney? If she'd stayed in Winchester she'd at least have been content, but now…

You're like a child, crying for the moon, her mind whispered as she slowly went downstairs. Be grateful for what you have—your children and your health. But I want more, her lonely heart whispered back. Suddenly, and crazily, I want more, much more. I want Michael.

# CHAPTER EIGHT

'THIS heat's not natural, love,' George Abbot declared as Bethany put one hand on either side of his calf and firmly began massaging upwards. 'Now, in the south of England—Devon, Cornwall, places like that—you expect it, but it's not natural to have weather like this in Orkney.'

Bethany blew a strand of hair off her cheeks, enjoying the momentary feeling of coolness against her skin, and nodded. Even with her electric fan switched to maximum, her consulting room was unbearably hot and had been for the last week.

'There'll be a storm before this day's over,' the retired fisherman continued. 'Best make sure you've plenty of candles in the house. Electricity's always the first thing to go in a storm.'

Bethany glanced out the window at the clear blue sky and unconsciously shook her head. Storm nothing. This hot, humid weather wasn't ever going to break, and certainly not today.

'How are you getting on with the cabbage leaves, George?' she asked, bringing her hands together round his thigh and easing the flesh up towards the top of his leg. 'Are you finding it any easier now you're blanching the leaves instead of ironing them?'

'Much easier.' He nodded. 'Before, I was either burning them because the iron was too hot or I wasn't making them soft enough. Now I just throw a couple of leaves into a pot, squeeze out as much water as I can when they're blanched and wrap them round my knees with a bit of cotton on top to keep them in place.'

'And the devil's claw?' she continued, helping him to

urn over so she could begin massaging the front of his leg.
Have you enough to last until your next appointment?'

'I have, worse luck,' he said ruefully. 'Lord, love you,
ear. It's like drinking sheep dip.'

She laughed. 'Well, you know what they say, George.
The more revolting a medicine tastes, the better it is for
you.'

'In that case, I should soon be running a four-minute
mile.' He chuckled. 'And talking about medicines…you
must have been gobsmacked when you found out Nora
Linklater had that disease—the one where folk deliberately
make themselves ill to get medical attention.'

Bethany's smile didn't slip for a second, but inwardly
she was seething. 'I'm afraid I can't discuss one of my
patients with you, George,' she said as evenly as she could.

But somebody had been prepared to hint at the truth, she
thought angrily, and she didn't need three guesses to figure
out who.

'Don't look a gift horse in the mouth, Bethany.' That
was all Michael would say when she confronted him with
it, and though common sense told her she shouldn't—especially when people were starting to make appointments
again—she couldn't deny she was angry.

And he knew it, too. He'd dropped by a couple of times
since she'd had dinner with him last week, and though he'd
been friendly and pleasant she'd had the distinct impression
that he was happier talking to Katie and Alistair.
Perversely, that only made her angrier still.

OK, not angry, she conceded as she began kneading
George Abbot's other calf. Jealous. Jealous of the sounds
of happy laughter drifting into the house from the garden,
jealous of Katie's and Alistair's all too obvious pleasure in
his company. And it was ridiculous. Being jealous of your
own children was just plain ridiculous.

'Had my six-weekly check-up with Dr Harcus the other

day,' George Abbot commented, almost as though he'[d] read her mind. 'He was greatly impressed with my knees.'

'That's good,' Bethany murmured absently.

'Nice bloke, Michael.' George shot her a sideways glance. 'Not lucky in love, though.'

'He seems to have been far too lucky, from what I'v[e] heard,' Bethany replied more tartly than she'd intended and heard George snort.

'That's not love, dear, that's sex. Love isn't about taking but giving. Love's about being there for the bad times a[s] well as the good. Michael never understood that before, bu[t] now... Now I think he does.'

The fisherman's keen blue eyes were fixed on her and [a] slow blush crept across Bethany's cheeks. 'George—'

'His sister would be over the moon if he decided to settl[e] down at last, and if he settled down with a ready-mad[e] family—'

'I think I might try you with some cinnamon as well a[s] the devil's claw,' Bethany said quickly, fighting down he[r] mounting colour. 'It's an excellent circulatory tonic—'

'So is a happy marriage, love.'

'George—'

'OK, I won't say another word,' he declared, his blu[e] eyes twinkling. 'But you could do a lot worse, you know.'

Of course she could, but Michael wasn't on offer. Jake on the other hand, to her stunned amazement had implie[d] that he might be. He'd phoned her twice in the last te[n] days, and by the time she'd put down the phone she'd be[-] gun to wonder whether they actually were divorced. It ha[d] been all 'darling this' and 'sweetheart that', as if all th[e] heartache she'd endured over the last five years had bee[n] nothing but a bad dream.

'He wants something, Bethany, so you be careful,' he[r] mother had warned when she'd told her, but she didn't nee[d] the warning. She didn't trust Jake as far as she could throw him. She was just curious to find out why he wanted to see the children now, of all times.

'It's not getting any cooler, is it?' Mardi complained when Bethany met her in the corridor after she'd helped George Abbot out to his car. 'I hope your ex likes hot weather or he'll fry when he arrives tomorrow.'

Frankly, Bethany didn't much care if Jake melted, but she didn't say so. The only reason she'd told her receptionist of Jake's imminent arrival had been in case she needed to reschedule some of her appointments, but that was as far as she was prepared to go in sharing confidences.

'When are the children due back from Kirkwall?' Mardi continued.

'Not until after ten. Connie said she'd take them to the cinema for a treat after they had their swimming lesson.'

'I'd cancel the cinema if I were you,' Mardi observed, glancing uneasily out of the office window. 'I think a storm's coming.'

'Good grief, not you, too.' Bethany laughed. 'The way everyone's carrying on this afternoon you'd think a hurricane was on the way.'

'But—'

'Has Helen Grayson arrived for her five o'clock appointment yet?' Bethany asked, deliberately changing the subject.

'Yes, but—'

'Send her through, please, Mardi.'

Her receptionist opened her mouth, then closed it again, and Bethany shook her head as she walked quickly through to her consulting room. Three of her patients had cancelled their appointments this afternoon because of this supposed storm, and she wouldn't be at all surprised if Helen Grayson cut her appointment short for exactly the same reason.

She did.

'I've only come because I've run out of peppermint capsules,' Helen said as she sat down, 'otherwise I'd have cancelled today for sure.'

'Are the capsules helping at all?' Bethany asked.

'A bit, but not as much as I'd hoped.'

Helen sounded depressed and Bethany wasn't surprised. Irritable bowel syndrome was a surprisingly common affliction, affecting one person in ten, but nobody was very sure why the peristalsis—the wave-like action of the gut that propelled faeces towards the rectum—became irregular, causing erratic bowel movements with constipation, diarrhoea and abdominal pain. All anyone knew for certain was that, once affected, a patient could suffer periodic bouts for years.

'Would you be willing to try a tea made of goldseal, German chamomile, wild yam, agrimony and marshmallow?' she asked as she counted some capsules into a bottle. 'Some of my previous patients found it greatly reduced the contractions of the intestinal muscle.'

'Frankly, I'd be prepared to stand stark naked in my garden for a couple of hours a day if I thought it would get rid of this condition,' Helen sighed.

'I think we'd better try the tea first.' Bethany chuckled. 'But if that doesn't help there are still lots of things we could try. The main difficulty with irritable bowel syndrome is getting the right balance of herbs. Too much agrimony, for example, can worsen your condition, whereas too little would mean you'd see no improvement at all. How are you getting on with massaging your stomach?'

'Much better since you gave me that tape to listen to while I'm doing it. And now, if you don't mind, I really must go,' Helen continued. 'I promised my husband I'd be home—'

'Before the storm breaks,' Bethany finished for her wryly. 'What is it with everyone today? There's not a cloud in the sky or a breath of wind, and there was no mention of bad weather on the weather forecast.'

'We don't put much faith in forecasts in Orkney,' Helen declared as she walked to the door. 'In Orkney we go by the animals and birds, and they've been skittish all day.'

Once Helen had gone, Bethany sent Mardi home too. It seemed pointless to keep her when she had no more patients, and it also meant that she could enjoy the luxury of having the house all to herself for the evening.

But, try as she might, she couldn't enjoy it. Every time she sat down her treacherous thoughts kept drifting to Michael, and every time she got up she'd trip over something of Katie's and find herself thinking about the children.

She'd told them Jake was arriving tomorrow and neither of them had said a word. Not a why, or a when, or a what for. They'd simply exchanged glances, then pleaded homework they needed to finish. Their silence had made her edgy, uncomfortable. The silence outside the house tonight was even eerier. Presumably this was the lull before the storm, she thought wryly as she ate her dinner. Even more probably everyone was panicking about nothing.

By ten o'clock she took it all back. By then the wind was wailing like a demented banshee around Sorrel Cottage, buffeting the walls and rattling the windows, and torrential rain was pouring off the gutter. She'd often wondered why the houses in Orkney were built looking away from the stunning sea views, instead of facing them. Now she knew. If Sorrel Cottage had been facing Eynhallow Sound she wouldn't have had a window left.

'Of course I'll be all right on my own,' she told Connie after she phoned to say she wasn't going to risk driving the children home that evening. 'And I'm not on my own—I've got Tiny here to protect me.'

Who was about as much use as your typical average male in a crisis, she thought ruefully as she put down the phone and stared at him. At the first rumble of thunder he'd dived into his bed and refused point blank to come out again.

'You're supposed to be protecting me, you stupid dog,'

she exclaimed, flinching as yet another fork of jagged light ning split the sky. 'How are you going to do it from i there?'

Tiny wagged his tail in reply, then promptly retreate even further under his blanket as they both heard the soun of someone banging vigorously on the front door.

'That could be an axe murderer or a rapist for all w know,' she told him. 'Aren't you even going to bark?'

He clearly wasn't and, grumbling quietly to hersel Bethany walked swiftly to the front door, to discover nei ther an axe murderer nor a rapist outside, but Michael.

'I'm sorry to disturb you,' he gasped, pushing his han through his soaking wet hair, 'but I've been out on an emer gency and I was on my way back to Kirkwall when swerved to avoid hitting a stupid sheep and crashed the ca into a wall. Can I use your phone to call the garage? M mobile doesn't seem to be working.'

'Of course you can,' she replied, ushering him in quickl before the door was torn from its hinges. 'But are you OK Are you hurt in any way?'

'I'm fine,' he replied dismissively. 'I just need to get hol of Eric and hopefully I'll be on my way.' But when h picked up her phone they discovered it wasn't working ei ther. 'Some telephone wires must have snapped somewher down the line,' he observed. 'I'm afraid it looks like you'r stuck with me for the night.'

'Stuck with you?' she said. 'You mean…you mean yo want to stay here?'

Her dismay must have been all too apparent because h coloured slightly. 'Look, if it's a problem I'll walk on t the next house—'

'Don't be ridiculous,' she protested, pulling herself to gether. 'I wouldn't ask my worst enemy to walk anothe two miles on a night like this!'

His mouth slanted into a wry smile. 'Care to rephras that?'

Not really, she thought. 'Would you like something to eat?' she asked instead. 'I could heat up some soup, or make you a salad. I just wish I had some dry clothes to offer you but I've nothing that would fit. There might be an old sweater of Jake's somewhere—'

'Bethany, I'm fine,' he said gently as she half started towards the door. 'All I need is a towel and maybe a coffee.'

Of course he did, she thought as she retrieved a towel from the airing cupboard, and yet she was clucking round him like a headless chicken. Calm down, Bethany, she told herself, calm down. So he has to stay here tonight. So what? It's no big deal. You've got plenty of empty bedrooms with the children away, and just because he's standing there looking so damn big, so male, so...

'Are the children in bed?' Michael asked, rubbing his wet hair vigorously as he followed her into the kitchen.

'They're in Kirkwall with Connie. She was taking them swimming tonight, then to the cinema, but the storm broke, and...' She shrugged. 'I just hope Katie's not being too troublesome. She's never spent a night away from home before.'

'They'll be fine,' he declared. 'Connie's very good with children.'

'So are you,' she said without thinking as she spooned some coffee into a cup. 'In fact, Connie said...'

She came to a sudden, embarrassed halt and his face creased into a smile. 'Don't hold back on my account, Bethany. Just what—exactly—did my little sister say?'

Bethany hesitated for a second, but only for a second. 'That you were very much in love with a girl called Sarah Taunton, but it didn't work out.'

'Yes, and no. Yes, it didn't work out and, no, I wasn't very much in love with her.' His smile widened. 'You're curious, like everybody else, about why I don't date any more.'

'I'd say that was pretty much your own business,' she replied, handing his coffee and wishing she'd never started this conversation.

'I don't date any more because I suddenly realised that chasing a whole lot of women was something I should have outgrown years ago.' He took a sip of his coffee. 'I stopped dating when somebody told me I had no heart.'

'But that was a horrible thing to say—and completely untrue,' she protested. 'You've been kindness itself to me and the children.'

'Ever wondered why?'

His deep brown eyes were fixed on her over the rim of his cup and, try as she might, she couldn't look away.

'Because— Well, because you're a very nice man,' she faltered.

'Am I?' His voice was a soft caress, a caress that curled down deep inside her, and she gripped the edge of the kitchen table tightly, all too aware of her fast beating heart and his closeness in the silence.

And it was silent, she suddenly realised. Eerily so.

'It…it looks as though the worst is over,' she managed to say. 'The storm, I mean.'

'Bethany, it's hardly started yet. In fact, you're lucky to still have electricity.'

As though on cue the lights immediately flickered and went out, and she scrabbled quickly in one of the kitchen drawers. 'It's OK. I have candles in here somewhere…'

She felt rather than saw him shake his head. 'Take my tip—buy some hurricane lamps tomorrow. Buy a lot of hurricane lamps tomorrow.'

'Do you think the electricity will be off for long?' she asked as she handed him a candle balanced somewhat precariously in an egg cup.

'It could be five minutes—it could be all night. It depends on what's gone down.'

His eyes were still on her and her breath caught in her

roat. It was like being in Maeshowe again, she thought s the candle flame illuminated his face, making it all dark lanes and shadows, only this time it was ten times worse. his time she knew exactly what the feel of his lips on hers vould be like. This time her lips were aching—yearning— or that touch, and it was crazy, crazy.

'If the electricity's going to stay off perhaps we should ust to go to bed,' she blurted out, then blushed scarlet as he realised how that sounded. 'I mean—I meant—we ould trip over something—'

'I know what you meant, Bethany,' he interrupted softly.

Thank God one of them did, she thought, forcing herself o walk past him out of the kitchen. Right now her brain idn't appear to be in any kind of working order at all.

'The spare bedroom's made up,' she continued as she ed the way upstairs, 'but I'm afraid I don't have any py-amas that would fit you.'

'It doesn't matter. I don't normally wear any.'

She stumbled slightly at that bit of news but managed to ceep on walking. So he slept in the nude—so what? robably lots of people did. Yes, but lots of people aren't Michael, her mind whispered. Lots of people don't have houlders like a barn door, and a chest like…

Pull yourself together, woman, she told herself sharply s she ushered him into the spare bedroom, then fled to the afety of her own room. If you don't watch out you'll be hrowing yourself into his arms, and do you really want im laughing at you—do you? Just get into bed and sleep, nd in a few hours it will be morning, and he'll be gone.

But she couldn't sleep. How could she with the rain and he wind roaring around the chimneys? she asked herself s she watched the bedside clock slowly record the passing ours. But it wasn't the wind and rain, and she knew it vasn't. It was the thought of Michael sleeping along the passage from her. Michael, wearing nothing at all. Michael, ust a few footsteps away.

Stop it, she told herself, rolling over onto her side as the luminous dial on her clock showed five o'clock and she thumped the pillow for what must have been the hundredth time. You're a grown woman, for God's sake, not a teenager with a crush. In a few hours he'll be gone, and—

The blast of thunder exploding overhead had her sitting bolt upright. The sound of breaking glass somewhere in the house had her scrambling out of bed and out into the passage. Not her treatment room, she prayed. Please, make it anywhere in the house but my treatment room.

'I think it's your bathroom window,' Michael exclaimed, appearing without warning at her side. 'I can feel a draught.'

So could she and she started forward immediately, only to feel his hand on her arm. 'Watch out for broken glass, Bethany. If the window's gone there'll be shards everywhere.'

There were, and tears filled her eyes when she surveyed the mess. The curtains she and Katie had specially chosen in Kirkwall were ripped to shreds, the bathroom cabinet she'd lovingly painted lay smashed on the floor, and the bath had all but disappeared under a collection of splintered wood and glass.

'Leave it to me, Bethany,' Michael said, hearing the sob she couldn't suppress. 'I'll do what's necessary.'

And he did. Using a blanket from Alistair's bed and the staple gun Bethany had been using to make a pelmet for the spare bedroom, he tacked a temporary barrier over the gaping hole. It wasn't perfect, but at least it would keep out the worst of the wind and rain.

And it was then, without the wind whipping her hair across her face and the rain half blinding her, that she suddenly realised what he was wearing. The old wrap-around dressing-gown she kept in the spare bedroom. A wrap-around dressing-gown that ended halfway up his arms and barely covered his muscular thighs.

He should have looked ridiculous—he *did* look ridiculous. She should have felt like laughing. She didn't.

Instead, she swallowed hard as she realised that her thin cotton pyjamas were clinging like a second skin to her damp body, and he'd noticed.

'I'd better— W-we ought to get back to bed,' she faltered, crossing her arms instinctively across her breasts.

He nodded slowly, his eyes following her action, dark and deep and unfathomable.

'We could still grab an hour's sleep,' she continued. 'You've got to go to work this morning, and I…I have a pretty busy day ahead, what with Jake arriving, and my patients, and…'

She was babbling, she knew she was, but never had she been so aware of a man. Never had she wanted anyone as much as she suddenly wanted him.

She wanted to press herself against him. She wanted to lay her head on his shoulder. She wanted—oh, dear God, how much she wanted—to have his hands touch and caress her, to assuage the ache she felt in her breasts and to ease the pulsing, slippery rush between her legs, and it was madness, insanity.

'I…we ought to get back to bed,' she said, backing away from him. 'You're working tomorrow— I mean today. You need your sleep—and I…I…'

'What? What do you need, Bethany?' he said, his voice thick, hoarse.

She couldn't answer him. The words just wouldn't come, and before she could move he reached out and slowly began to take the pins from her hair. 'You have no idea how long I've been wanting to do this,' he said, his voice little more than a whisper as he threaded her hair through his hands and onto her shoulders.

A shiver ran through her that had nothing to do with the cold. 'Michael, don't. Please—'

His lips captured her protest—lips that teased, and

coaxed, and tempted—but still she tried to fight against her feelings even when she realised that somehow they were in her bedroom.

'Michael, we shouldn't be doing this,' she gasped, her arms snaking of their own accord around his neck as he brushed her forehead then the fluttering pulse at her throat with his lips.

'I know,' he muttered, gently unbuttoning her pyjama top.

'Michael, I'm sure—if you thought rationally—you'd realise we really mustn't do this,' she moaned as he cupped her breasts in his hands and bent his head towards them.

'Who wants to think rationally at a time like this?' he asked raggedly, drawing one nipple into his mouth and suckling it into an aching hardness.

'Michael…oh, Michael this is crazy—ridiculous,' she protested, digging her fingers deep into his shoulders when he turned his attention to her other breast.

'Isn't it, though,' he answered, sliding her pyjama trousers slowly down.

I ought to stop him, she told herself as his hands and mouth paid homage to every inch of her throbbing body. I ought to be sensible, she thought as he rolled her on top of him to cup and caress her buttocks, bringing her hard against him so she could feel his own arousal. But by the time he slid her under him again she didn't want to be sensible any more. All she wanted was an end to the frantic need that was consuming her.

'Michael, please…please…' she begged, and while she was still dazed with the feelings he had already awakened in her he gently eased inside her.

And it *was* all exploding bubbles and rainbows when he began to move, hard and deep, inside her. It *was* all soaring crescendos and pulsing, throbbing lights, so that when he arched above her and cried out, a deep guttural cry of elation, her own cry mingled with his at the sheer wonder of the sensations that had engulfed her.

Slowly, gradually, her breathing returned to normal and her heart rate steadied, and she opened her eyes to find his brown ones fixed on her.

'Are you OK?' he murmured.

OK? She felt incredible, wonderful, but she managed to reply a little raggedly, 'Yes…Yes, I'm fine.'

'Oh, Bethany, don't,' he said in dismay. 'Please…please, don't cry.'

She hadn't even realised she was, and she smiled up at him tremulously. 'I'm OK—truly, I am. I just…I just…'

How could she tell him she was crying because no one had ever made her feel like this before? How could she say she wanted him to hold her and never let her go? He'd think she was mad, but what *did* you say to someone you'd just made love with? Made love with not because it had been planned, or because you'd intended to, but because it had just happened.

*Was it good for you?* That was cringe-making. *I'd like to do this again some time.* That was even worse.

She wished she was experienced. She wished she hadn't done it. No. No, she didn't wish that, she thought as she gazed up at him, seeing the concern, the uncertainty, in his deep brown eyes, but what *did* you say after the deed was done? Could you ask outright whether this meant the start of a relationship, or would that be considered too forward, too intense?

Ye gods, how much more forward can you get? a little voice demanded at the back of her mind. You've just made love with him, haven't you?

She cleared her throat, then to her relief she heard Tiny barking downstairs. 'I think he wants out.'

'I'll do it,' Michael replied, throwing back the duvet.

'But you've got no clothes on—'

He didn't even answer. He simply strode out of the bedroom without a backward glance, grabbed his clothes from the spare room and went downstairs. And it was only when he was standing, shivering, on the doorstep while Tiny sniffed up and down the garden, looking for that one, special place to do his business, that he wondered what the hell he was doing down there.

You're here because you panicked, he realised. You're here because for the first time in your life this isn't a game any more.

In the past it had always been so easy with the women he'd made love to. A brief kiss afterwards, a warm smile that could mean anything and generally meant nothing, and then he was gone with no thoughts of tomorrow. But what did you say to someone you'd just made love with when you knew without a shadow of a doubt that you loved them? Loved them with a depth and fervour you'd never experienced before?

*Will you marry me?* Hell, if he said that she'd think he'd lost his mind. *Can we do this again some time?* That sounded too casual, too indifferent, and he felt anything but indifferent.

He should have stayed in bed with her. He should have pulled her into his arms and made love to her again, and then he wouldn't have had to say anything.

Had he pleased her? He thought he had but, then, why had she cried? Had she regretted what she'd done—or, even worse, had he disappointed her?

Play it cool, Michael, a little voice advised at the back of his mind as he heard the sound of her footsteps in the hallway. Wait and see what she says, what she does, then take your cue from her. The one thing you mustn't do is burden her with your feelings, embarrass her with a declaration of love that she can't return.

'The electricity's back on,' she murmured awkwardly, 'and my phone seems to be working again.'

'Your phone?' he said blankly.

'Won't you need to contact the garage to organise a breakdown lorry for your car?'

He'd forgotten all about his car, frankly didn't care if he never ever saw it again. 'Bethany…'

He came to an uncomfortable halt, not knowing what to say, and Bethany felt her heart twist inside her.

He regrets it already, she thought as she gazed at him and saw the faint flush of colour on his cheekbones. In the cold light of day he can see what you are, who you are, and the thought of having even a brief affair with you horrifies him.

A sob welled in her throat and she desperately crushed it down. Somehow she had to salvage something out of what had just happened even if it was only her pride. Somehow she had to convince him that when they'd made love… Oh, God, when they'd made love she'd felt safe for the first time in years. Safe, and cherished and protected, but that wasn't what he wanted to hear, she knew it wasn't.

'Michael, there's no need for you to say anything,' she said swiftly as he cleared his throat, clearly unsure how to begin. 'I understand—I do. You're not into commitment, and certainly not to a thirty-three-year-old woman with two children and stretch marks.'

'I love your stretch marks,' he protested, 'and I adore Alistair and Katie—'

She put her hand to his lips to silence him and smiled, a small crooked smile that tore at his heart.

'Michael, it's all right—truly it is. We both got a bit carried away—the storm, the circumstances. What we did…' She swallowed hard. She was going to say this if it killed her. 'We really mustn't read any more into it than there actually was.'

He gazed at her speechlessly. It was so ironic, so damned ironic. He'd said the same thing himself to so many women in case one night of passion might have been interpreted as some kind of commitment he'd never intended making.

And now for the first time in his life he wanted a woman, not just physically but to be a part of her life, to be there for the small things in life as well as the big, and she was telling him she didn't want that.

'Bethany, listen—'

'You'd better phone the garage, and go back to your car to wait for Eric,' she interrupted. 'Connie will be bringing the children back home to catch the school bus and, though explaining your presence to them wouldn't be difficult, Connie's an entirely different kettle of fish.'

She turned to go, and he threw caution to the wind. 'Bethany, there's something I have to tell you. Something you must know—'

'I haven't time right now, Michael,' she interrupted swiftly, knowing that the last thing she wanted to hear from him was how he'd always respect her, how they'd always be friends. 'I've got to get dressed and ready for work, and I want to clean the house before Jake arrives this afternoon.'

'But, Bethany—'

He'd caught hold of her arm and she jerked herself free. 'Feel free to make yourself some breakfast before you go, but please… Please, don't be here when the children get back.'

And she walked out of the kitchen, feeling her heart splintering into tiny pieces with every step, and didn't know that he gazed after her. Didn't know that he watched her until she disappeared from sight, then swore, long, and low, and fluently.

# CHAPTER NINE

'BOY, but was last night wild, or what?' Mardi exclaimed with feeling as she hung up her coat and shook the rain-drops out of her hair. 'Our chimney went at four this morning, Mrs Fraser across the road lost her barn roof, and...' She came to a halt and frowned. 'Hey, are you OK, Bethany? You're looking a bit peaky this morning.'

'I'm fine,' Bethany replied with an effort. 'Just a little tired, that's all.'

'I'm not surprised,' her receptionist observed. 'I doubt if any of us got any sleep last night. Have you phoned the glazier and joiner about your window? They're bound to be bombarded with calls after last night, and...'

How could she have been so stupid? Bethany wondered as Mardi chattered on, and she smiled and nodded, and didn't hear a single word the girl said. Everyone had warned her about Michael, had told her he could charm any woman he wanted out of her knickers, and yet she'd fallen for him like everyone else.

And not just fallen for him. God, she'd even persuaded herself she would accept an affair with him, and what had she got instead? A one-night-stand. How could she have been so naïve? How could she have been so stupid?

'And you know what men are like.'

'I do?' Bethany faltered, and her receptionist shook her head and chuckled.

'I don't believe you've heard a word I've said! I was just saying that the white willow you gave Eric really seems to be helping his back. He's still in pain, but at least he doesn't look like the hunchback of Notre Dame any more so with two weeks to go there's a chance our wedding and honeymoon won't be a complete wash-out.'

Her honeymoon with Jake hadn't exactly been memorable, Bethany recalled, but when she'd made love with Michael…

No, she wasn't going to think about that, she told herself. In fact, she was never going to think about Michael Harcus ever again.

'Bethany, are you sure you're OK?' Mardi frowned. 'Do you want me to phone Dr Harcus, ask him to come out and see you?'

Not if she'd been bleeding to death, and he'd been the single solitary person in the world who could save her.

'I'm fine, Mardi,' she said firmly. 'Was there something else?' she added as she half turned to go, and the girl cleared her throat awkwardly.

'It's a bit embarrassing really,' Mardi began, flushing deeply. 'And, like I told Eric, I'm sure you've just forgotten.'

'Forgotten what?' Bethany said, puzzled.

'That you haven't paid his last garage bill yet.'

She hadn't forgotten. She just didn't have the money to pay it.

'Please, give Eric my apologies,' she replied, hoping she didn't look as guilty as she felt. 'It's just I've had so many things on my mind lately, what with Jake coming this afternoon, Nora Linklater—'

'That's what I told him.' Mardi beamed. 'Will I tell Eric you'll be paying him soon? I know he'll be really grateful.'

And I'll be downright amazed, Bethany thought as she nodded. Maybe if they stopped eating for the rest of the week, and maybe if she did some part-time housebreaking she might be able to come up with the £300 she needed but unless she could screw some money out of Jake she had about as much hope of paying Eric's bill as sprouting wings.

Why, oh, why did everything have to be such a mess? she wondered as she went through to her consulting room. She was up to her ears in debt, Jake was arriving in less than six hours and the children had made it all too plain that they didn't want to see him, and Michael...

How in the world was she ever going to face him again? Orkney was so small that she was bound to meet him, to see him, and how could she do that, feeling the way she did about him, knowing he didn't care for her in return?

Get through today, she told herself, stiffening her spine as she heard a car arriving outside the cottage and knew that her first patient of the day had arrived. Somehow get through today, and then you can think about tomorrow, and then all the tomorrows after that, in the knowledge that it can't get any worse.

She was wrong.

It was after John Russell left with his monthly supply of feverfew leaves for his migraines that Mardi popped her head round the door to ask if Alistair could have a word with her before she saw her next patient.

'You mean he's still home?' Bethany exclaimed in surprise. 'What happened—did he miss the school bus?'

'I don't know. The only thing he'd tell me was that he wanted to see you urgently.'

Urgently? She'd give him urgently, Bethany thought grimly. When they'd lived in Winchester her son had made a habit of truanting, but she'd thought the move to Orkney had put a stop to it. Now it seemed as though it was starting all over again.

'Go easy on him, Bethany,' her receptionist said, seeing her expression. 'He really does seem to be upset about something.'

The imminent arrival of his father no doubt, Bethany realised with a groan. Katie had only been thirteen months old when Jake had left and couldn't remember him at all, but Alistair had been almost five and, judging by the belligerent expression he'd been wearing ever since she'd told him his father was coming, he was going to make the visit as difficult as possible.

'OK, Alistair, what's the problem?' she said with a sigh as she opened the kitchen door and saw him standing by the window, staring out at the garden. 'If it's about your father coming—'

'Michael was here last night, wasn't he?'

'W-what?' she stammered, totally thrown by the unexpected question.

Her son's chin wobbled for an instant, then firmed. 'Michael—he spent the night here, didn't he?'

'Well, yes, he did,' she replied, striving to sound casual, dismissive. 'He had an accident in the storm, and had to shelter—'

'In your bed?'

Scorching colour lit up Bethany's cheeks. 'Alistair, that's ridiculous—'

'Is it?' he said, his small lip curling.

'Alistair—'

'I found this in your bed,' he declared, producing Michael's distinctive Rolex watch from his pocket. 'How did it get there if he wasn't in there with you?'

'What were you doing in my bedroom in the first place?' she demanded, desperately trying to buy herself time to think.

'Does it matter?' he asked, his pale face furious. 'We get sex education at school—I know what he was doing there with you, and it's…it's gross!'

'Alistair, listen—'

'Isn't it bad enough my father's coming here this afternoon, but you have to be stupid enough to go and get involved with another man?'

'Alistair, Michael and I are not involved. We…he…' Oh, Lord, she could hardly tell her own son that last night had been nothing more than a one-night-stand. He already knew

o much, without him knowing the whole sorry details.
He... We...'

'He'll make you cry, like Dad made you cry. I remember
,' he continued as she gazed at him, horrified. 'I remember
ou yelling at Dad, and him yelling at you, and then you
rying.'

'Alistair—'

'I'm not a little kid. I can take care of you—look after
ou. We don't need somebody else coming along, spoiling
everything, hurting you.'

'Alistair, listen to me,' she began slowly. 'Nothing is
oing to change. Michael... He's a...a friend—nothing
ore. He isn't going to be moving in, or taking over, or
hanging anything.'

'You say that now,' he insisted, 'but I've seen the way
ou look at him.'

Dear God, was her face really so transparent?

'How I look at him is immaterial,' she forced herself to
eply. 'Alistair, you have my word—my solemn pledge—
at Michael and I are not going to get involved with each
ther.'

'But you'd say yes if he asked you, wouldn't you?'

She would, she thought wretchedly. Oh, yes, she'd say
es in a minute. 'Alistair, I thought you liked Michael—'

'You *are* going to get involved with him!'

'Alistair, I'm not—'

'I don't want to hear any more—I don't want to listen
 anything you have to say about Michael,' he cried, run-
ing for the door.

'Alistair, come back!'

But he didn't. He just took off along the corridor, with
iny careering madly after him, and then the front door
ammed shut.

For a second she half started after him, only to stop.
eave him to calm down, her mind urged. You'll get no-

where when he's so angry and upset. Leave him to calm
down, and then hopefully you can talk to him.

And say what? she wondered. That his mother was a
fool? That her taste in men was lousy? That her heart was
breaking because she'd fallen in love, and the man she
loved didn't love her back?

She couldn't say that, she just couldn't, but she was going
to have to tell him something.

Mardi was waiting for her, looking deeply embarrassed
and uncomfortable, when she came out of the kitchen. 'Mrs
Allison's here, Bethany. Will I tell her you've got family
problems, that you need to cancel her appointment?'

How much her receptionist had heard was anyone's
guess, but she'd clearly heard enough, and Bethany shook
her head.

'It's OK, Mardi, it will sort itself out.' She took a deep
breath and tried to smile. 'Everything sorts itself out in
time.'

She just wished she could make herself believe it as the
morning dragged by and she got through her consultations
on autopilot. How could she stay on in Orkney, never seeing
Michael again or—even worse—seeing him at a function,
remembering what they'd shared, remembering how
stupid she'd been?

Women get dumped all the time, Bethany, her mind
pointed out. You're not the first, and you certainly won't
be the last. Jake dumped you, and you survived that. But
this is different, her aching heart cried. This time it isn't
just me who's hurting but Alistair, too—and what about
Katie? She'd grown so fond of Michael, and if she wasn't
able to see him any more, she'd ask questions—questions
Bethany didn't want to answer.

Then the only thing you can do is leave Orkney, her
mind whispered. Cut your losses, sell the cottage and leave,
but that prospect only made her feel even more wretched
than she already did.

'Bethany, I'm getting really worried,' Mardi said the minute she had shown her last patient out. 'It's almost two o'clock and Alistair's not come back yet.'

'Not back?' she gasped. 'But he left—'

'Over four hours ago.' Mardi nodded. 'Do you think he's all right?'

She didn't. Alistair had taken off before but never in such a blazing temper, and never for so long. A cold chill gripped her heart as she remembered something else. Alistair might have been away for four hours, but he hadn't eaten for at least six.

Swiftly she reached for the phone.

'Are you calling Michael?' Mardi asked, her plump face creased with worry.

Bethany nodded. Six hours with no food meant that Alistair's glucose level must be low. Six hours of running about, using up energy, meant that his glucose levels must be dangerously low… Phoning Michael might be awkward and embarrassing, but right now she didn't care how awkward it was. She needed help, and he was the best person to give it.

'It's OK, Bethany, Michael's here!' Mardi exclaimed just as the number began to ring, and without a second's hesitation Bethany was out of the office and running to the door to meet him.

'Bethany, I had to come back, to speak to you,' he said as soon he got out of the car. 'There's something I have to say even if you don't want…' He came to a halt and scanned her face. 'What is it? What's wrong?'

'It's Alistair. We had a huge row this morning and he took off with Tiny and hasn't come back.'

He could hear the blind fear in her voice, her desperate attempt to disguise it, and his fingers tightened round hers. 'Bethany, boys of his age do that all the time. Once he's cooled his heels—'

'But, Michael, it's hours since he ate anything. Even if

he remembers to take his insulin, he won't have had any food, will he?'

Which meant that unless they found Alistair, and quickly, he could become hypoglycaemic and go into a coma.

'Why the hell did he just take off like that in the first place?' Michael shot out, worry making him angry. 'He's not a baby. He knows he must eat regularly, so what the hell made him do it?'

She didn't want to tell him what she and Alistair had been arguing about. She'd have given anything in the world not to tell him, but she knew she must. 'Michael, he went because...because he knows you were here last night— what we did.'

He stared at her blankly for a second, then shook his head. 'He can't—'

'Michael, he *knows*.' She squeezed her eyes tight shut as though to contain the pain. 'He was so angry, so hurt. Oh, Michael, if anything's happened to him, I'll never forgive myself.'

Neither would he. Dear God, did the boy hate him so much? Was the idea of him and his mother as a couple so repugnant to him? He'd come back this afternoon as soon as Eric had arranged a hire car for him, determined to tell Bethany how he felt, but if Alistair was prepared to put his life in danger at just the thought of them together...

'Do you have any idea where he might have gone, Bethany?' he asked, forcing himself to sound calm for her sake.

A sob came from her as she shook her head. 'He was always going off by himself exploring, you know that.'

He frowned deeply, then his eyes lit up. 'Birsay. You know how fascinated he is by the Vikings, and most of the ruins on the island are Norse. I'd bet money he's gone to Birsay.'

'And it's a tidal island connected by a path to the main-

and,' she exclaimed, a glimmer of hope appearing in her eyes. 'You think the tide might have changed, and he's stranded there?'

He nodded, but he didn't tell her what had also occurred to him. That though a concrete path led across the rocks to the island it would be treacherous after all the rain they'd had, and if Alistair had tried to come back when the tide was turning, with his glucose levels falling…

'Where are you going?' he demanded as she slipped her hands from his and began walking towards her car.

'To Birsay—to look for him.'

'I'll take you.'

'But you must have patients to see,' she protested. 'I can't ask you—'

'You didn't,' he said, then smiled slightly as he remembered the first time he'd said that to her.

She remembered it, too. He could tell by the faint tinge of colour that appeared on her cheeks, but she didn't say anything. She simply walked to his hired car and got in.

They drove in complete silence to Birsay, the only sound being the constant sweep of the windscreen wipers on the window, and Michael prayed as he had never prayed before. Please, Lord, let the boy be all right or Bethany will never be able to bear it. Please, Lord, I'll never ask for anything else again if you'll only let the boy be all right.

And Bethany prayed, too. Prayed that the bitter words Alistair had thrown at her wouldn't be the last she'd ever hear him speak. Prayed that he was just stranded and cold and miserable, and not lying somewhere, slipping into a coma. The wind of last night might have dropped completely but it hadn't stopped raining, and if Alistair was on Birsay, unconscious, with only his school uniform for protection…

'There's no sign of him, Michael,' she exclaimed in panic when they reached the headland. 'The tide's come in, but I can't see him anywhere!'

'He could be sheltering in one of the ruins,' he replied hoping to God it was true. 'In this weather, it's what I' do.'

'But how are we going to get over there to find out she demanded. 'Should we—?'

'Can you hear a dog barking?' he interrupted.

She strained her ears but all she heard was the patter the rain on the grass. 'I can't hear anything.'

'Listen!' he commanded, and finally she heard it. Fain hoarse, but unmistakably the sound of a dog barking from somewhere nearby.

They slipped and slid their way down the bank, follow ing the direction of the sound, and eventually, after wh seemed like an eternity, found Alistair lying huddled besic some rocks, with Tiny standing guard over him.

'Sorry...so sorry, Mum,' he mumbled when she kne beside him. 'The tide...the causeway... I fell. My leg...s sore...so sore.'

'He's hypoglycaemic, isn't he?' she asked, biting her li savagely to keep her tears at bay when she saw the bead of sweat on her son's forehead, the way he was shudderin and trembling.

Michael nodded and swiftly took a syringe out of h bag. He had to get some hormone glucagon into the bo and fast. If the brain didn't receive sufficient glucose could lead to permanent mental impairment, but there wa no way he was going to tell Bethany that.

'I'm just going to give you an injection, Alistair,' he sai rolling up the boy's sodden sleeve. 'So I want you to rela Relax...relax... Terrific.'

'Should his face be quite so puffy?' Bethany asked wi concern.

It shouldn't, not if Alistair was simply hypoglycaemi He seemed drowsy, too, and though that could just hav been due to his low glucose levels, something told Micha that it wasn't.

Quickly he felt under the boy's armpits and his groin. They should have been warm—they weren't.

'Wrap your scarf round his head, Bethany,' he ordered as he pulled his sphygmomanometer out of his bag and began taking Alistair's blood pressure.

'His head? You think he's injured his—?'

'We lose twenty per cent of our body heat through our heads,' he interrupted. Damn, but the boy's BP was low, too low. 'I think Alistair might have a touch of hypothermia.' Which had to be the biggest understatement of the year, he thought grimly.

'Hypothermia! Michael—'

'It's nothing to worry about,' he interrupted, smiling across at her with an optimism he was very far from feeling. 'No, don't do that,' he added quickly as she began chafing Alistair's cold hands between her own. 'It's the worst possible thing you can do for someone with hypothermia. That, and letting them walk, or giving them hot drinks and a hot-water bottle. We need to get his temperature up very slowly.'

'I'm sorry. I didn't realise—'

'There're some blankets in the boot of my car,' he interrupted, slipping off Alistair's wet sweatshirt and replacing it with his own sweater. 'Could you go and get them for me?'

She didn't want to go—he knew she didn't—and, judging by the speed with which she came back, he guessed he'd run the whole way.

'How is he?' she asked, her face white, her eyes strained.

'His sugar levels are going up and his blood pressure seems to be going down. No, don't do that yet,' he said when she began tucking one of the blankets round her son. 'I think he may have broken his leg to add to his troubles, and I'll need to splint it first.'

Tears began to trickle slowly down her cheeks. 'I...I can't do anything right, can I?'

'Bethany—'

'I'm supposed to be able to help people,' she continued 'but when it comes to my own son…'

Michael gripped her tightly by the shoulders. 'Bethany you told me yourself that herbalism works best with long term, chronic ailments—'

'I know,' she sobbed, 'but I feel…I feel so damn *useless*!'

'Bethany!'

He glanced warningly down at Alistair, and she dashed a hand across her cheeks and took a shuddering breath. He was right. That was all her son needed right now—her falling apart.

'I'm sorry, I'm sorry,' she mumbled. 'I just… What do you want me to do?'

'Find me some driftwood. Something long and straight I'll splint his leg, and then we'll get him to hospital.'

The driftwood she found wasn't ideal but it sufficed, and with the leg splinted and Alistair wrapped in the blankets Michael drove like the wind to Kirkwall Infirmary.

'He will be all right, won't he, Michael?' she couldn't help but say convulsively when the staff in the Accident and Emergency unit whisked Alistair out of sight. 'He isn't going—?'

'No, he's not,' he said firmly, and prayed with all his heart that it was true.

Their wait for news seemed endless but, in fact, it was only a little under an hour before one of the doctors came to see them.

'We've put your son's leg in plaster, Mrs Seton, and at the moment we've got him in a warm bath to raise his temperature slowly. All in all, I'd say he's got off pretty lightly. We'll have to keep him in, of course, to make sure there are no complications, but I don't anticipate any.'

'Thank you,' she whispered. 'I don't know what else to say, but thank you.'

The doctor grinned. 'Don't thank me. Just be grateful
you had Michael with you. He did one hell of a job.'

And with that, he was gone.

'I told you he'd be fine, didn't I?' Michael smiled, un-
crossing the fingers he'd been keeping crossed behind his
back.

'I know, but—'

'I wouldn't lie to you, Bethany.'

No, he wouldn't lie to her, she thought, not about
Alistair. She'd seen the way he'd carried her son to his car,
so gentle, so protective, and the way Alistair had clung to
him, his anger and resentment temporarily forgotten.
Michael would never lie to her about Alistair.

Limply she sat down, and Michael scanned her face in-
decisively. She looked like hell, and he didn't want to add
to her distress, but there was something he had to ask,
something he had to know.

'Bethany, does Alistair hate me so very much?'

She stirred uncomfortably in her seat. 'Michael, do we
have to talk about this right now?'

'I know it's not a good time,' he agreed, 'but Alistair...
I thought he and I were friends, that he liked me.'

'He does, but...' She stared at the floor, quite unable to
meet his gaze. 'He's afraid. He thinks...he thinks you're
going to hurt me.'

She didn't hear him move, yet suddenly he was standing
in front of her.

'And you, Bethany?' he murmured, his voice low, deep.
'What do you think?'

That you've already hurt me, she thought, noticing ab-
stractly that his shoes were wet and muddy, his trousers
salt-sprayed. You've already made me feel like a fool. But
she wasn't going to tell him that, didn't even want to discuss it. 'Michael, I don't think this is the time—'

'Bethany, when...when I made love to you...' He
paused, cleared his throat and started again. 'Bethany, I

know I have a dreadful reputation. I know any sane woman would run a mile from someone like me, but…'

She made the mistake of looking up at him, and was lost. 'But?' she echoed faintly.

'This morning I knew…' He shook his head. 'No, dammit, I knew a long time ago.'

'Knew what?' she whispered through a throat so tight it hurt.

'I knew—' He broke off with a muttered oath as suddenly the door of the waiting room swung open and a blond-haired man appeared.

Bethany didn't swear, but her mouth certainly dropped open. '*Jake*—what in the world are you doing here?'

Apart from displaying the worst timing in the world, Michael thought with frustration as Jake Seton strode towards them.

'I went to your house when I got off the boat, and your receptionist said Alistair's had some sort of accident. Is he all right? I was so worried—'

'Well, that's got to be a first,' she snapped before she could stop herself. 'Our children could have been hospitalised innumerable times over the last five years for all you knew, or cared.'

Way to go, Bethany, Michael thought exultantly as Jake reddened. Tell the jerk where to get off, to get out of your life for keeps.

'What happened to him?' Jake asked.

'He broke his leg, and because he was lying out in the cold for so long with no food he became hypoglycaemic and got hypothermia, too,' Bethany replied.

Jake whitened. 'Hypoglycaemic? You mean, he's a diabetic?'

'If you'd stuck around long enough, you'd know that, Jake,' she retorted.

'Bethany, can't we leave the past in the past?' he murmured in a tone that made Michael feel slightly sick but then, he was a little bit biased. OK, he was very biased. 'I made a mistake when I walked out on you—a big one—and, believe me, I've paid for it. Can't you find it in your heart to forgive me?'

'Jake—'

'I'm not the man I was. I've changed.'

Wanna bet? Michael thought sourly. Men like Jake didn't change. They might say that they had, they might even promise that they would, but they never did.

'I've been a fool—a blind, stupid fool,' Jake continued. 'I walked away from the best things in my life, but I want to make it up to you—to the children. Dammit, the children are my own flesh and blood, and when I think of Alistair lying in a hospital bed...'

He was getting to her, Michael could see it. 'Look, I hardly think this is the time or the place to be attempting a reconciliation,' he said acidly.

'Who is this?' Jake demanded, glancing at Michael with ill-concealed annoyance.

'Michael Harcus—a friend,' Bethany replied.

'And I was your husband for seven years,' Jake declared. 'Don't I merit a little privacy?'

She supposed he did and reluctantly she glanced across at Michael. 'Would you mind leaving us alone for a few minutes?'

He minded like hell. He wanted to pick Jake up by the scruff of the neck and run him out of the hospital and out of Bethany's life, but he managed to say, 'I'll wait outside by the car.' Then he banged out of the waiting room, seething inwardly.

'You look tired, Bethany,' Jake said as soon as they were alone.

He meant old, she thought, her gaze taking in his immaculate clothes and his suntan, which clearly hadn't come out of a bottle or from a sun-bed but from a couple of weeks on some exotic beach. Well, maybe if she'd had more than a pittance to live on for the last five years, and a holiday once in a while, she'd look as good as he did.

'It was a bit of a shock, seeing where you and the children live,' he continued.

'A shock?'

'I'm sure it's very healthy, being so close to the sea and all,' he added hurriedly, seeing her defensive expression, 'but it's…well, it's a bit basic, isn't it?'

'Considering you never send me any money—'

He held up his hands to silence her. 'Bethany, can't we let bygones be bygones? We had some good times together when we were first married.'

'But the children arrived and spoilt everything—is that what you're saying?' she said, failing to keep the edge out of her voice.

'No. *No*,' he repeated vehemently. 'I thought they had—I admit it. I was too immature to see that, though they had changed our marriage, it was a good change. Bethany, I treated you and the kids badly, but I want to make it up to you.'

'Sending me some money regularly would certainly be a big help,' she replied, thinking of Eric's garage bill and all the other unpaid bills in her desk.

Jake gazed at her awkwardly. 'That's not what I meant. Bethany, I want you and the children to come and live with me again, for us to be a family again. I love you all, and I've never stopped loving you.'

She gazed at him silently. The nerve of him—the sheer, unmitigated nerve! Did he really think it was that easy? Did he really think he could just waltz back into her life, wearing his little-boy-lost look, promising to solve all her financial worries, and she'd forgive him everything?

OK, it might be wonderful to be able to open the mail in the morning and not be confronted by a mass of bills. And it would be even lovelier to be able to give the children

ll the things she could only dream of, but she didn't trust
ake any more, and she certainly didn't love him.

'Sweetheart, you don't have to come to any decision im-
nediately,' he said, clearly reading her mind. 'I'm going
o stay in Orkney until I'm sure Alistair is on the mend, so
ou don't have to come to any snap decision. All I'm ask-
ng is for you to give me a chance.'

You had it five years ago, Jake, she thought as she made
or the door. 'I have to go. I want to see Alistair, then I
nust get home for Katie.'

'But you'll think about what I said?' he pressed.

'Oh, I'll think about it, Jake,' she replied as she walked
ut of the waiting room. Think about how I once loved you
ut you let me down, and I can't ever forgive you for that.

Michael was standing by his car as he'd promised, Tiny
appily asleep in the back seat. 'Alistair OK?' he asked.

'A lot better than I expected,' she replied.

'Good.' He nodded, and for the first ten miles of the
ourney back to Evie he managed to restrain his curiosity,
alking about the staff at the Infirmary and the physiother-
py Alistair would require once his plaster was off. For the
next five miles he talked about mutual patients, but when
e saw Sorrel Cottage on the horizon he could bear it no
onger. 'And how's your ex?'

'Full of plans.'

'Plans?' He shot her a glance. 'What sort of plans?'

'He… He wants me to go back to him, wants us to be
family again.'

'I see.' That was all he could reply, completely stunned.

Was that all he was going to say? Bethany wondered,
taring across at him. OK, so he didn't love her, but
ouldn't he at least tell her not to be a fool, that Jake was
user and a taker—or was he simply too uninterested to
are?

Ask him, her mind urged. Don't just sit there, wonder-
ng—ask him.

'Michael, what do you think I should do?' she force
herself to say.

'It's up to you, Bethany.' Oh, hell, why had he said that
It made him sound like he didn't care—and he did care
desperately. 'I mean—what I meant is, it's not really fo
me to say.'

Oh, God, that sounded even worse, he realised, as thoug
he were indifferent to her decision.

What was wrong with him? he wondered as he stoppe
the car outside her cottage and turned to face her and saw
how pale and weary she looked. He never used to have
trouble with words. Hell, he used to be able to twist any
woman he wanted round his finger if he put his mind to it
but with Bethany… He sounded so cold, so uncaring, and
that was the last thing he felt.

Tell her you love her, you idiot. Tell her you'll spend
the rest of your life trying to make her and the children
happy.

'Bethany—'

'I'm sorry—I shouldn't have asked you that,' she inter
rupted, quickly undoing her seat belt and opening the door
her face averted. 'It isn't your problem.'

'But, Bethany—'

'I can't thank you enough for what you did for Alistair
and I won't ever forget it.'

'Bethany, wait!'

But she didn't wait, and he hadn't really expected her
to. Why the hell would she want to stay and talk to some
one who had just proved himself to be, yet again, a genuine
grade A, insensitive idiot?

# CHAPTER TEN

'PITY the weather's been so foul since your husband arrived,' George Abbot declared as Bethany helped him down from the massage table.

'Ex-husband, George, not husband,' she replied, waiting until he was steady on his feet before walking over to her desk and taking out his prescription. 'I've made you up some more devil's claw for your knees—'

'I understand he's leaving today?'

'That's right. Now, about the devil's claw—'

'The word is that you might be leaving Orkney, too.'

Her head came up in amazement. 'Who on earth told you that?'

'I get around,' the retired fisherman replied. 'In fact, I also heard that you're planning on remarrying your ex.'

Bethany shook her head and smiled. 'It's amazing what people find to talk about.'

'Would the word be wrong, then?' George asked, his deep blue eyes fixed on her.

'About remarrying my ex—absolutely wrong,' Bethany declared, closing her desk drawer with a bang.

'And about leaving Orkney?'

Lord, was her home bugged? She'd told no one but her mother that she'd been to an estate agent to discuss putting Sorrel Cottage on the market, and yet it appeared that everyone knew about it already.

'Is it true?' George pressed, and Bethany managed to laugh.

'George, if you were a woman I'd say you were a terrible gossip.'

He chuckled, too, but he didn't give up. 'Seems like a huge waste of two lives to me.'

'I expect Jake will survive,' she replied lightly. 'Now, I've made your devil's claw slightly weaker this time—'

'Wasn't meaning your ex, dear. I was thinking of somebody a whole lot closer to home. Michael Harcus, in fact.'

'George—'

'In fact, I'd say that if ever two folk were smitten with each other, it's you and Dr Michael.'

'That's ridiculous,' she protested, all too aware that her deepening colour totally contradicted her words, and George shook his head.

'Look, dear, I may be retired but I'm not blind, deaf or senile. The man's in love with you, and I think you're in love with him.'

'George, this isn't—'

'Any of my business?' A wide smile lit up his weathered face. 'Of course it isn't, but I like you both, and I think you'd be a fool to leave when he so clearly loves you.' .

'If he does, he's got a funny way of showing it,' Bethany retorted tartly before she could stop herself.

'What do you want him to do?' George demanded. 'Hire an aeroplane to write your name in the sky? Take out a full page spread in *The Orcadian*, listing his intentions?'

'I want…' She swallowed the hard lump which always came to her throat whenever she thought about Michael. 'If he really loves me, I want him to tell me so.'

George sighed. 'If you're waiting for that, dear, you're going to still be single when you're as old as me. The man's got his pride. He's not going to tell you he loves you if he thinks you might turn him down.'

'Then what am I supposed to do?' she protested.

'Ask him if he wants you to stay.'

'You mean, I should go up to him, throw my arms around his neck and say, "Look, you idiot, I'm in love with you"?'

'Something like that—though I'd forget about throwing
our arms around his neck if I were you.' George grinned.
Reckon you'd need to take along a stepladder to do that.'

'George, I couldn't,' Bethany said in horror. 'What if he
laughed at me? What if he said, "Hey, that's nice to know,
but I don't love you"? I'd never be able to hold my head
up again.'

'That's your pride talking, love.'

'Maybe it is.' She nodded. 'But my pride's the only thing
I've got left right now.'

'Listen to me, dear—'

'No, George,' she interrupted firmly. 'You're a kind man,
and you mean well, but I have to handle this my own way.'

And she did, she thought as she showed the retired fisherman out. Jake had been on the island now for almost a
fortnight and Michael hadn't dropped by once. He'd
phoned Mardi to ask how Alistair was when he'd come out
of hospital, but he hadn't asked to speak to her, hadn't even
mentioned her.

Well, she could take the hint. He'd wanted her on the
night of the storm, but he didn't want her now.

Which meant she had two choices. She could stay on in
Orkney, accepting that she would see him occasionally at
functions with all the heartache that would entail, or she
could leave the island and start again.

Actually, she had a third choice, but she wouldn't have
entertained Jake's offer even if she and the children had
been homeless and destitute. Not when she'd found out that
the only reason Jake wanted her and the children back was
because he'd been offered a job working for an American
TV company. A company that put great store by old-
fashioned family values.

'You're a fool, Bethany,' Jake had said, his eyes showing
both rage and total bewilderment when she'd told him in
no uncertain terms what she thought of his offer. 'I could
give you and the children everything!'

Yes, but for a price she wasn't prepared to pay, she thought. To live with a man she no longer trusted, let alon loved, was far too high a price to pay.

'You're sure you won't need me this afternoon?' Mard asked as she came out of her office.

Bethany smiled. 'Absolutely. I deliberately made sure only had morning appointments so I could take the childre to Stromness to see Jake off.'

'I'll be amazed if you can get them anywhere near th harbour,' Mardi commented as she slipped on her coat.

So would Bethany. Jake's visit had been anything but comfortable one. Alistair had spent the whole time scow ing at him, and Katie had hidden behind her skirts, her gre eyes wide and uncertain once the novelty of entertaining visitor had worn off.

'How are you getting on with your wedding arrang ments, Mardi?' she asked, swiftly changing the subjec 'You've only got four days left before the big one.'

'Don't I know it,' the girl groaned. 'But at least Eric back is fine now. In fact, Dr Harcus said he'd never see anyone make such a quick recovery.'

It would have been nice if he'd told her so, Bethan thought as she watched her receptionist drive away, b presumably phone calls were out of the question now, well as visits.

Stop it, Bethany, stop it, she told herself, feeling a te trickle down her cheek. You weren't going to think abou Michael, remember? You've managed to squeeze enoug money out of Jake to pay most of your outstanding bill including Eric's, and you've been to the estate agent to se about putting the cottage on the market, so look forwar and not back.

But I love him, her aching heart cried as she walked bac into the house and along to the kitchen. It wasn't the kin of love she'd felt for Jake when they'd first got married– that desperate, blind passion which had fizzled out whe the realities of life crept in. She wasn't blind to Michael's faults. She could probably have named every single one of them, and yet…

Yet she loved him, loved him with every fibre of her being, and he was never going to love her back, never going to want her, no matter what George Abbot believed, and she was just going to have to accept it.

'Shouldn't you two be getting ready to go?' she said with a frown when she opened the kitchen door to find Alistair and Katie sitting at the table, apparently deeply engrossed in jigsaws. 'Your father's ferry leaves in less than two hours—'

'We don't want to see him off.'

Her son's still too-pale face was belligerent, Katie's was determined, and Bethany groaned inwardly. She'd expected Alistair to dig in his heels, but not an all-out mutiny.

'Look, if you won't do it for yourselves, can't you do it for me?' she begged. 'Your father came all this way—'

'We didn't ask him to,' Katie interrupted.

'I know you didn't,' Bethany said as calmly as she could, 'but he's going home—back to London. Is it too much to ask that you both just go down to the harbour?'

'To wave bye-bye and make like we're all one big happy family?' Alistair shook his head. 'I'm not going, and neither is Katie. We phoned Aunt Connie and she said we could stay with her this afternoon if you agree.'

Bethany glanced from Alistair's belligerent face to Katie's determined one. She couldn't make them go. She couldn't drag them, kicking and screaming, to Stromness. Jake would be furious when they didn't arrive. He'd blame her—say she was turning the children against him—but she would just have to put up with it and endure his anger.

'OK,' she sighed in defeat. 'You can stay at Connie's this afternoon, but if I'm dropping you off in Kirkwall before going on to Stromness, you'd better get moving.'

To her surprise neither child moved. Katie gazed point-edly across at her brother and he cleared his throat.

'Everyone's saying we're leaving Orkney.'

'Look, I don't have time to discuss this right now,' Bethany replied, inwardly cursing the Orkney grapevine. 'We can talk about it tonight or tomorrow—'

'I don't want to leave Orkney,' Katie declared, her small jaw setting into a stubborn line. 'I like it here. I've made friends at school, and Aunt Connie is great, and Michael—'

'Katie—'

'I don't want to leave either,' Alistair chipped in. 'This is our home now, and you're getting more and more pa-tients so I don't see why we have to go somewhere else.'

'Alistair—'

'If you make us leave we'll hate you for ever and ever!' Katie cried.

Bethany gazed at her helplessly, then at her son. 'Alistair, surely you understand?'

'No, I don't,' he said. 'You like it here, too, I know you do. Is it because of what I said about Michael?'

'What did you say about him?' Katie demanded, her small brows lowering, her jaw jutting out in clear prepa-ration for battle. 'What did he say about Michael, Mummy?'

'It doesn't matter,' Bethany declared swiftly. 'Alistair—'

'I didn't mean it,' he interrupted. 'I'm going to apologise to him the next time I see him. I think he's OK really, and if you want to marry him—'

'Mummy's going to marry Michael?' Katie's face lit up with such pleasure that Bethany's heart twisted inside her. 'Can I be a bridesmaid and wear a red dress with tartan ribbons—?'

'Katie, I am not going to marry Michael,' Bethany pro-tested. 'I don't know why Alistair's got such a crazy idea into his head, but I am not—most definitely *not*—ever go-ing to marry Michael Harcus!'

Two pairs of mutinous eyes stared up at her. Two pairs
' eyes that also looked hurt and disappointed. Then
listair slipped from his seat. 'Come on, Katie. If we're
)ing to Aunt Connie's, we'd better start getting ready.'

'Alistair!'

He didn't even turn round at Bethany's call, but Katie
d. 'I think you're mean,' she announced. 'I'd like to have
lichael as a daddy, and so would Alistair, and I think
)u're mean and…and *horrid*.'

And I want to go down to the health centre in Kirkwall
ıd pummel Michael Harcus senseless, Bethany thought as
ıe listened to the children's feet clattering on the stairs,
ıen the sound of their bedroom doors slamming.

He'd waltzed into her life, made her fall in love with
ım, made the children grow fond of him, and now he'd
altzed right out again, leaving her to pick up the pieces.
/ell, she'd rebuilt her life once before when Jake had left.
he would leave Orkney, find a new home and start again.
he would have to, she thought as she wearily gathered up
ıe scattered jigsaws on the kitchen table. There was noth-
ıg else she could do.

1ichael walked past the whitewashed Tankerness Museum
ıd the rose-coloured façade of the St Magnus cathedral,
ıen cut down Albert Wynd to the health centre. Nothing
ad changed in Kirkwall since he'd been a boy. The names
ver the shops were the same, the people he passed were
ıe same. He could probably have walked down Albert
/ynd blindfolded and not got lost, and yet suddenly, shat-
ringly, nothing was the same any more.

Don't think about her, he told himself as he stopped out-
ide the health centre to gaze at the stormy, rain-tossed
aters in the harbour and found himself picturing
ethany's face. Bethany, looking pale and unhappy.
ethany, with the wind blowing in her hair, her eyes alight

with laughter. Bethany, in his arms, her cheeks flushed, h
lips slightly parted.

Stop it, he told himself, just stop it. You can't mak
somebody love you, so chalk it up to experience and mov
on, forget her. You're Michael Harcus, remember. Micha
'Mr No Commitment' Harcus. And an empty, hollow ma
he thought with a deep sigh as he opened the door of th
health centre and went inside.

'Looks like we've got a full house this afternoon, I
Harcus.' Rose beamed when she saw him.

Wall-to-wall patients would be a more accurate descri
tion, Michael thought with an inward groan. 'Has Simo
arrived yet, Rose?'

'He arrived ten minutes ago, Doctor.'

Michael nodded, half turned on his heel, then paused an
wrinkled his nose. 'Is it my imagination, or is there a ver
strong smell of lavender and eucalyptus in here this afte
noon?'

His receptionist coloured slightly. 'I've got a slight col
Doctor, and I heard— I read somewhere that lavender an
eucalyptus were very good for getting rid of colds.'

'Seems to me you're not the only person who read th
article,' he said, grinning. 'The whole place reeks of th
stuff. Where did you read such nonsense?'

Rose coloured still further. 'I didn't actually read it.
happened to meet Bethany Seton in the street...' Her voic
faltered as his eyebrows snapped together. 'It can't do an
harm, Dr Harcus.'

No, it couldn't do any harm, he thought as he turne
abruptly and strode into his consulting room, but did ev
erything and everybody have to keep on reminding him o
Bethany?

You're going to have to get used to it, his mind pointe
out. Unless you're planning on leaving Orkney, you're go
ing to have to get used to people talking about her. An
not just talking about her. Unless you're going to becom

a hermit, there's every chance you'll see her in the street, meet her at some function, so, for God's sake, get a grip.

But it was easier said than done when his first patient turned out to be Linda Balfour.

'I'm surprised to see you, Linda,' he said when she sat down. 'I thought you were quite happy with Mrs Seton's treatment for your CFS.'

'I am. In fact, whether it's because of the herbs I'm taking or whether it's due to the massages she's giving me, I have to say it's a long time since I've felt so well.'

'Then…?'

'What am I going to do when Bethany leaves?' Linda demanded. 'The nearest herbalist and aromatherapist is in Thurso on the mainland, which means a boat trip—'

'Leaves?' he repeated. 'Mrs Seton is thinking of leaving?'

'Marie Lattimer, who works in the estate agent's in town, told me Bethany came in last week to see about putting her house up for sale. I thought you'd know all about it, Dr Harcus,' Linda added in surprise, 'what with you and Bethany being such good friends and all.'

'No. No, I didn't know,' he murmured.

'Well, you can see the fix I'm in,' Linda said. 'If Bethany's treatment is helping me, I don't want to stop, but—'

'Leave it with me,' he interrupted quickly. 'I'll…I'll sort something out.'

Linda didn't look convinced, and Michael couldn't blame her, but his mind was in too much of a whirl for him to make himself sound convincing.

He'd told himself that it would be hell bumping into Bethany unexpectedly, but that didn't mean he wanted her to leave!

Where would she go—what would she do? He knew she didn't have much money, and the thought of her and Katie and Alistair moving to the mainland, living in some grotty bedsit somewhere…

'Mrs Robson to see you, Dr Harcus.'

That was all he needed this afternoon, he thought with a deep groan as Rose's voice came through the intercom. His sister bending his ear, plaguing him about Bethany, but Connie didn't look in a belligerent frame of mind when she breezed into his consulting room. In fact, she looked terrific. Her eyes were glowing, her cheeks had a soft, luminous quality to them, and she was smiling at him as though she'd just won the lottery.

'What can I do for you, Connie?' he asked as she sat down.

'Eat a very large slice of humble pie for starters,' she declared.

'Humble pie…?'

Her smile widened. 'I'm pregnant, Michael. I wanted you to be the first to know after Simon and me. I'm pregnant.'

He gazed at her, stunned, for a second, then shook his head in disbelief. 'Connie, are you sure?'

'With a doctor for a husband you bet I am.' She laughed. 'Simon and I did the test yesterday, then we did it again this morning, and it came up positive each time.'

He let out a whoop of delight which must have caused quite a bit of comment outside in the waiting room, but he didn't care. 'Oh, Connie, I'm so pleased for you—so very pleased. How far on are you?'

'Eight weeks.'

'Which means the baby will be born some time in April,' he said, doing some rapid calculations. 'We'll have to get you signed on at the clinic, make sure you're taking all the right vitamins. You'll need to book a midwife, too, and no more taking Benjie for long walks—'

'Slow down, slow down,' his sister said, chuckling. 'I've got a long way to go yet.'

'But you're happy?' he said softly.

Her lips trembled for a second, then she smiled. 'Do you have to ask? And it's all because of Bethany's treatment.'

If he'd wanted to be churlish he could have told Connie she would probably have conceived perfectly naturally without Bethany's herbs and oils, but he didn't want to be churlish. In fact, if he was going to be really honest with himself, he truly didn't know any more.

'I owe Bethany a lot,' Connie continued, as though she'd read his mind. 'So do you, Michael.'

'I'll drop her a line—thank her,' he said evenly.

'You'd better do it fast because I understand she's leaving,' she said, her eyes never leaving his face.

'So I've heard,' he replied, forcing himself to sound casual, dismissive.

'Is that all you're going to say?' Connie protested. 'Are you telling me that you're going to let the best thing that ever walked into your life walk right out again, without even putting up a fight?'

'Connie—'

'Michael, it's obvious to anyone with half a brain that you're in love with Bethany. Why the hell don't you just tell her?'

'Because…' He paused and when he spoke again his deep voice was edged with roughness. 'Because I don't want to burden her with something I know she'd rather not hear.'

Connie threw her eyes heavenwards with exasperation. 'God, give me strength. Of course she wants to hear it, you big ninny!'

He shook his head, his mouth curved into a slightly bitter smile. 'Believe me, Connie, she doesn't.'

'What does she have to do to prove it?' his sister asked in exasperation. 'Buy a megaphone and shout her love for you in the middle of Kirkwall on a Saturday morning? Phone up Radio Orkney and ask them to broadcast it? Michael, a woman has her pride.'

'And a man has his.'

His sister's eyes narrowed. 'I never thought you were a coward, Michael.'

'A *what*?' he gasped, his eyebrows snapping down.

'You heard me,' his sister continued, meeting him glare for glare. 'For God's sake, stop being terrified of being knocked back. Stop dithering about, wondering if this is the right time or that is the right time. Just tell Bethany you love her and want to marry her.'

'Yeah, right,' he said scornfully. 'And look a proper idiot when she tells me she doesn't want to marry me.'

'I'll eat my hat if she says that, but if she does at least you'll know you've tried,' Connie said. 'God knows, you've wasted too many opportunities already. Just tell her how you feel or you'll lose her for sure.'

He gazed at her for a moment, then kissed her lightly on the cheek. 'Don't forget to register for the antenatal clinic on your way out, Connie.'

'Michael, listen—'

'And it's wonderful news about the baby. I couldn't be more thrilled.'

His sister ground her teeth, then her head came up. 'OK, if you want to be a fool, then so be it, but I can't help feeling sorry for Katie and Alistair. Bethany might think she and Jake can make a go of it the second time round—'

'What the hell are you talking about?' Michael demanded, catching hold of his sister's arm as she made for the door. 'Bethany would never go back to Jake in a million years!'

'She *is* going back. In fact, she and the children are leaving with him on the ferry this afternoon from Stromness.'

For a second he looked stunned, then shook his head. 'I don't believe you. Bethany would never do anything so stupid.'

'Believe what you like, big brother,' Connie replied, shrugging herself free from his grasp with a glint in her eyes which she hoped he didn't see. 'I have to admit it's not what I'd have advised her to do, but she's in a mess financially, and I understand Jake is very well off…'

She couldn't be so stupid, Michael told himself. Nobody could be that stupid.

They could if they were desperate, a little voice at the back of his mind pointed out. They could if they felt there was nothing else for them to do, nowhere else for them to go, and nobody else they could turn to.

But there was somebody else Bethany could turn to. He'd promised her that, and he wasn't going to let her down.

Quickly he strode out of his consulting room and along to Reception. 'Rose, I have to go out.'

'Out?' she repeated, bewildered. 'Out where, Doctor?'

'Stromness.'

'But you have a waiting room full of patients—'

'Simon will take care of them,' he threw over his shoulder before he banged out of the door.

'Simon will take care of what?' his brother-in-law asked in confusion, emerging from his consulting room, clearly having been drawn by the sound of Michael's voice. 'What's happened? Is there some emergency?'

'Not as far as I know, Dr Robson,' Rose declared, bewildered. 'Dr Harcus was seeing your sister, then he suddenly upped and left.'

Simon turned to see his wife standing in the middle of the corridor, and fixed her with an accusatory stare. 'OK, Connie, what have you been up to?'

'Me?' she exclaimed, opening her eyes very wide. 'I haven't done anything.'

'Connie?'

'OK, all right, so maybe I might just have given Michael a little nudge,' she protested, 'and he'll thank me for it when he gets to Stromness.'

'Will he?' Simon demanded, and Connie giggled.

'Either that, or he'll murder me.'

'Cutting it a bit fine, aren't you, Doc?' The harbourmaster grinned as Michael abandoned his car and raced through the puddles on the quay towards the *St Ola*. 'The ferry leaves in ten minutes.'

'I'm not travelling today, Jack. I just need to speak to Mrs Seton urgently,' he gasped. 'Have she and her children gone on board yet?'

The harbourmaster frowned. 'I haven't seen the children, Doctor, but Mrs Seton's certainly about. Look, there she is—at the bottom of the gangway, just getting ready to board.'

Michael had also seen her, and without a second's thought he ran towards her, grabbed her firmly by the shoulders and spun her round to face him. 'Bethany, you are not getting on that boat, do you hear me?'

'Michael—'

'I don't care what Jake has said about him having changed. I don't care what he's promised you. You are *not* getting on that boat!'

'Michael, I've no inten—'

'I love you. Do you hear me?' he cried as she gazed up at him, startled. 'I think I've loved you from the very first minute I saw you, and I'm not going to let you walk out of my life without a fight. I know I haven't got the most wonderful reputation—'

'That's putting it mildly,' she murmured, her lips curving.

'But I've changed. Knowing you has changed me. I adore Katie, and Alistair—'

'He told me he's sorry for what he said. He didn't mean it.'

'I don't want his apology!' He thrust his hands through his wet hair desperately. 'Bethany…Bethany, I love you, and I know I'm never going to love anyone else as much as I love you. Jake's not good enough for you.' He shook his head, a wry smile flickering briefly. 'Hell, I'm not good enough for you either but, please…please, promise me you'll stay for a little while. Give me a chance. I can make you happy, I know I can. Don't get on the ferry. Don't…please, don't leave me.'

'Michael, I'm not getting on the ferry,' she said softly.

'You mean, you and the children are following Jake later, when you've sold the house?' he said as the gangway of the *St Ola* was pulled aboard and the anchor reeled in.

'No, I don't mean that.'

'You mean…' Oh, God, he knew he would never be able to bear it if Jake had decided to move here to stay here with Bethany. 'Jake's selling up in London, coming north?'

Bethany turned to watch the ferry ploughing out of Stromness harbour, foam flecking her white sides, seagulls squawking raucously in the grey sky. 'No, he's not selling up.'

'Then I don't understand,' he said in confusion. 'What are you going to do?'

The wind and rain was blowing stray tendrils of hair across her face, hiding her expression. 'Stay right here, I guess,' she murmured.

'You mean you're not leaving at all—you never had any intention of leaving?' he faltered.

'Oh, I thought about leaving all right,' she replied. 'Not with Jake—I would never have gone back to Jake—but I did think of moving somewhere else, starting again. But now…now I've decided I'm staying right here.'

He bit his lip, all too aware that the dark colour suffusing his cheeks had nothing to do with the wind blowing off the sea. 'I've just gone and made a complete fool of myself, haven't I?'

She turned towards him. He looked lost, and unhappy, and uncertain, and she didn't think she had ever loved him

as much as she did right now. 'That largely depends upon
whether you meant what you just said.'

'What I just said?'

'Something about having loved me from the very first
minute you saw me but that you weren't good enough for
me?'

The colour on his cheeks darkened to crimson, but he
couldn't take back what he'd said—he didn't want to.
'Bethany, I want you to stay with me, I want you to marry
me. I know I'm not the children's father—'

'Anyone can be a father, Michael,' she interrupted. 'Jake
never understood that, but to be a dad… To be a dad takes
effort and commitment. It means being there for the bad
times as well as the good. It means enduring the drive-you-
up-the-wall occasions as well as the magical ones.'

'Are you saying…?' He swallowed with difficulty. 'Are
you saying you might consider staying with me?'

A smile lit up her face that all but took his breath away.
'Michael Harcus, I love you and I'd marry you tomorrow
if I could.'

For an instant he stared at her, as though not quite be-
lieving what she said, then with a cry that tore at her heart
he enveloped her in his arms and kissed her as though he'd
never let her go.

Dimly she heard whoops and catcalls coming from the
fishermen on their boats in the harbour, but she didn't care.
They could have hoisted the two of them aloft for all the
island to see, and she still wouldn't have cared. Michael
loved her. That was all that mattered.

'Why didn't you say something before?' she whispered
into his neck when he finally released her and she buried
her face in his shoulder. 'Why didn't you tell me you loved
me?'

'Because I was afraid,' he confessed. 'So afraid you'd
tell me you didn't love me—couldn't ever love me. You
seemed to want nothing but friendship from me—'

'Oh, I wanted a lot more than that, believe me.' She chuckled shakily. 'But I never thought you'd want me—a divorcee with two children.'

The smile on his face faltered. 'Bethany, about the children. Alistair—'

'He wants us to get married, Michael. So does Katie. In fact, they told me this morning that they'd hate me for ever if I didn't marry you.'

'Sensible kids.' He laughed huskily. 'Where are they, by the way?'

'With Connie. They didn't want to come to see their father leave, and I didn't want to force them.'

So Connie had known all along that Bethany and the children weren't leaving. He was going to wring her neck the next time he saw her. That, or buy her the biggest bottle of champagne he could find.

On second thoughts perhaps not champagne, remembering her pregnancy. He opened his mouth, intending to tell Bethany about it, then changed his mind. It would keep. A lot of things would keep right now except one.

'Bethany—'

'What about my herbalism, Michael? If I marry you—'

'*When* you marry me,' he interrupted firmly, and she laughed.

'OK, *when* I marry you, I couldn't give it up, stop practising.'

'I wouldn't expect you to,' he protested.

'And you won't interfere? You'll let me have my own patients, not sit on my shoulder like a broody hen as you've been doing these past few weeks with Linda Balfour?'

He opened his mouth, closed it again, then shook his head ruefully. 'I can't promise you that, but what I can promise is that if we ever argue about a patient, the making up afterwards will be truly memorable.'

'Really?' she said, her eyes dancing.

'Guaranteed,' he said with a nod, then cleared his throat.

'I know we haven't had a row, but you said the children were with Connie. What about Mardi?'

'I gave her the rest of the day off. She's marrying Eric on Tuesday, and she's still got lots to do.'

'Crazy.'

'Crazy?' she echoed, puzzled. 'Mardi having lots to do before her wedding is crazy?'

He shook his head, his lips curving. 'What's crazy is that your cottage is standing empty at the moment, and I'd like very much to show you how much I love you, and yet we're standing here, freezing to death, on this quayside.'

'So?' she prompted, her own lips curving in response to the love she could see in his deep brown eyes.

'Let's go home, Bethany.'

And they did.

# MILLS & BOON®

*Makes any time special*™

## Mills & Boon publish 29 new titles every month. Select from...

Modern Romance™          Tender Romance™

Sensual Romance™

Medical Romance™   Historical Romance™

MAT2

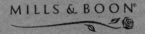

# MILLS & BOON®

# Medical Romance™

### A MOTHER BY NATURE *by Caroline Anderson*

*Audley Memorial Hospital*

Adam Bradbury is a gifted paediatrician and a devoted father. But he is sure that his inability to have children of his own will push any woman away. But Anna knows that Adam is wrong and she is determined to prove it...

### HEART'S COMMAND *by Meredith Webber*

Major Harry Graham had been drafted in to save the outback town of Murrawarra from torrential flood water but he hadn't bargained on Dr Kirsten McPherson's refusal to be evacuated...

### A VERY SPECIAL CHILD *by Jennifer Taylor*

*Dalverston General Hospital*

Nurse Laura Grady knew that her special needs son, Robbie, would always be the centre of her life. Could paediatric registrar Mark Dawson persuade her that he wanted both of them to be the centre of his?

## On sale 2nd February 2001

*Available at most branches of WH Smith, Tesco, Martins, Borders, Easons, Volume One/James Thin and most good paperback bookshops* 0101/03

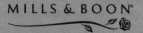

# Medical Romance™

**THE ELUSIVE DOCTOR** by *Abigail Gordon*

Ambitious Dr Nina Lombard did not want to be in the quaint village of Stepping Dearsley! But now that she was working for Dr Robert Carslake, Nina found that she had a reason to stay…

**A SURGEON'S REPUTATION** by *Lucy Clark*

Dr James Crosby has made his attraction clear to Dr Holly Mayberry but something from his past is holding him back. When James's reputation is put on the line Holly knows she has a chance to win his trust and his heart…

**DELIVERING LOVE** by *Fiona McArthur*

*New Author*

Poppy McCrae has always used complementary therapies in her work as a midwife. Paediatrician Jake Sheppard thoroughly disapproves of her methods. Can Poppy persuade Jake to accept her and her beliefs?

## On sale 2nd February 2001

*Available at most branches of WH Smith, Tesco, Martins, Borders, Easons, Volume One/James Thin and most good paperback bookshops*

0101/03b

# 4 FREE

## books and a surprise gift!

We would like to take this opportunity to thank you for reading this Mills & Boon® book by offering you the chance to take FOUR more specially selected titles from the Medical Romance™ series absolutely FREE! We're also making this offer to introduce you to the benefits of the Reader Service™—

- ★ FREE home delivery
- ★ FREE gifts and competitions
- ★ FREE monthly Newsletter
- ★ Exclusive Reader Service discounts
- ★ Books available before they're in the shops

Accepting these FREE books and gift places you under no obligation to buy, you may cancel at any time, even after receiving your free shipment. Simply complete your details below and return the entire page to the address below. *You don't even need a stamp!*

**YES!** Please send me 4 free Medical Romance books and a surprise gift. I understand that unless you hear from me, I will receive 6 superb new titles every month for just £2.40 each, postage and packing free. I am under no obligation to purchase any books and may cancel my subscription at any time. The free books and gift will be mine to keep in any case.

M1ZEA

Ms/Mrs/Miss/Mr ...........................Initials...........................
BLOCK CAPITALS PLEASE

Surname ...........................................................................

Address .............................................................................

..........................................................................................

..............................................Postcode...........................

**Send this whole page to:**
**UK: FREEPOST CN81, Croydon, CR9 3WZ**
**EIRE: PO Box 4546, Kilcock, County Kildare (stamp required)**